Who Killed The Warrior?

A New Beginning

Ras Iddi Wuni Jnr.

Order this book online at www.trafford.com
or email orders@trafford.com

Most Trafford titles are also available at major online book retailers.

Printed in the United States of America.

ISBN: 978-1-4669-1329-5 (sc)
ISBN: 978-1-4669-1331-8 (hc)
ISBN: 978-1-4669-1330-1 (e)

Library of Congress Control Number: 2012902703

Trafford rev. 07/16/2012

 www.trafford.com

North America & international
toll-free: 1 888 232 4444 (USA & Canada)
phone: 250 383 6864 ♦ fax: 812 355 4082

DEDICATION

In solemn memory of my late uncle, C.S Wuni (DC)

ACKNOWLEDGMENTS

First and foremost, to God be the glory. With Him, I am. Without Him, I am not. In Him, I trust. Praise be to thou Lord God.

My sincere thanks to the following people, my late uncle Rocks Gbanwaa for his book titled, The History of Bawku and the Senseless War, and also to Dr. Bateni Ayanaba of USA for his book titled, Memoir of Dr. Bateni. Your works have inspired me in accomplishing this dream. I would also like to thank Ena Bodh and Sheihu Milo for their help and prayers. Thank you my cherish reader for buying this book.

Last but not the least, to my mother Madam Binta Osman, "sweet mother I no go forget you for this suffer you suffer for me." Prince Nico Mbarga.

EPIGRAPH

"As far as I am concern, the light that I have lit in Africa will continue to burn and be born aloft given light and guidance to all even when I am dead and gone." Osagyefo Dr. Kwame Nkrumah, first president of the Republic of Ghana.

"I decided long ago never to walk in anyone's shadow if I fail. If I succeed at least I did as I believe." Whitney Houston.

CHAPTER ONE

CHIEFLY SEATED ON a lion skin on top of three large concrete stairs painted red, yellow, and green is the fifteenth chief of Zotinga, a descendant of Tohazie the red hunter. The rectangular prism stairs are constructed inside a 10'x 20' pavilion with side walls fencing it. The fence walls are two feet high and build with brown bricks measuring 21/4 x 33/4 x 8 inches. The ground floor is evenly leveled with sea sand and the pavilion roofed with locally made mat.

On top of the pavilion right in the middle of the roof is a dark earthen pot polished to look shinny and beautiful with fourteen white cowries glued around it. The fourteen cowries represent the past fourteen chiefs. Although the outside of it looks shinny and beautiful, no one knew what was inside it or how it appears in the inside.

He sat on the third stair and inscribed behind him on a white wall were names of his predecessors. Namely, Naa Ali Atabia *(1721-1732),* Naa Alibila Atabia Muzabaga *(1733-1747),* Naa Yakubu Atabia Mampanga *(1748-1753),* Naa Mahamadu Ali *(1754-1764),* Naa Mahama Mahamudu Sateem *(1765-1820),* Naa Baako Mahamadu *(1830-1843)* and Naa Mamboda Mahama *(1844-1894).* Beneath the name, of Naa Mamboda Mahama is a fine blue parallel line drawn and in the middle of it, is a white inscription, *The Bond of 1844 Chief.*

The names on the wall continued to appear as follows, Naa Mahama Mamboda Zangina *(1896-1908),* Naa Zangbeo Mamboda

(1909-1921), Naa Bugri Mamboda Lobzure *(1922-1935),* Naa Yakubu Mamboda Kuliga *(1936-1950),* Naa Wuni Bugri Saa *(1951-1956).* Beneath his name also is a blue parallel line with a white inscription, *Visionary and Selfless Leader of All Times.* It was during his reign that the Zotinga Hospital was built on a parcel of land he gave to the colonial masters for free of charge; not even a royalty fee agreement was signed. Naa Saa, the chief rain, as he was popularly known, was his nickname. As it is common with chiefs, he chose that name because he believes he symbolizes rain, and for that reason, there would be no drought in the village to prevent his subjects from farming. Next on the list after his name were Naa Yerimea Mahama Salima *(1957-1966)* and Naa Adam Zangbeo Tampuri *(1967-1981).* Bellow the name of Naa Tampuri on the list was the number fifteen, no name was attached to the number, and no period indicated. It was just two identical question marks (?-?). One representing name and the other one representing duration.

On the second stair right in front of him where the black star is artistically inscribed in the middle of the yellow color, are two little boys seated. They sat in a yoga bodily posture like Buddhist. Standing behind him also are two beautiful ladies fanning. They were as beautiful as a tropical water lily flower with a sweet smell of fragrance. To both his extreme left and right hand sides, seated forward in rows and close to the first stair are the elders. They sat in line of seniority. Also, standing behind them are the drummers. The chief linguist as usual, is standing in the middle, and the whole crowd at the palace added a touch of beauty to the ceremony.

The drums were painlessly crying even though the drummers were hitting with vigor. The dancers gleefully danced to the tune of the drums with pride, dignity, honor, respect and loyalty to the new chief. The elders watched them dance, and they were equally delighted and proud to see such a spectacular show of a cultural heritage which they have passed on to the young ones as it was passed on to them by their elders. It certainly reminded most of them of their youthful days. The smiles on the faces of the dancers as they happily danced attracted the admiration of the onlooker. The spectators just glued to their seats, and even those standing were not bothered about how long it might take them standing provided they could continue to see such a beautiful and skillful display of dance. The women also sang along just to motivate the men to dance.

"This is what we called '*damba.*' It's our cultural dance, our heritage our pride and our identity as a people. We trace our roots to Tohazie, the red hunter as I have told you already. Damba is the arts and manifestations of the wisdom, tradition and intellectual achievement of my people regarded collectively since the seventeenth century. It's usually celebrated in the month of February. Look in front of the palace. Can you see the flag with the photograph of an elephant embodied on it? It symbolizes the wisdom of our king. The other one on your left with a lion on it also represents the strength of all those who traced their roots to Tohazie, the red hunter. As you can see on the wall where the names are, our motto is *Gbegin wung lobzuri ka toz na yirigi,* which means, a lean lion has swung its tail and the chief hunter is scared. We the Mawus are a great people, and we traced our anthropological lineage to a brave warrior who was also a fearless hunter," Bachela explained to his guest.

Very much like his father, he looked skinny in his thirties. Measuring five feet eight and weighing about one hundred and fifty-five lbs. He is agile and fit. At the age of forty-five, he became an attorney out of a genuine desire to fight for justice, liberty and equal rights for the people of Zotinga. As an attorney, he founded the BaFa Group of Attorneys Law firm and was without a peer especially, in the area of civil rights and liberty law. As a young attorney he was not so much into criminal law as he was with civil and liberty law even though, he seemed sometimes comfortable handling criminal cases. Sometimes he will just handpick a few of the high profile political coloring cases just for their political value.

He was an astute lawyer and many admired the use of his legal skills in bringing people together.

He wore an honest face; a true reflection of the character inherited from his father. In a suit, he looked like a man who glanced at a mirror very seldom and his briefcase was like an ID badge, always in his right hand; an identification which is very common not only with most attorneys but, also with the politicians and a few of the 'Gold Coast business executives.' In the 17th century his ancestral forefather, Tohazie, was well known by everyone near and far. He was best described as a legendary superman, mystically powerful, a daring hunter and a brave warrior as well. His braveness and daring instinct was likened to the gross strength of ten vexed lean lions. The red hunter was also known to be most loathsome to behold, very revolting in character and also outstanding especially among his peers. It is said that, his name was so given in reference to his light-skinned complexion and his profession as a hunter.

As a warrior and a hunter, it is believed that he did dwell alone sometimes for many months in a grotto near a goddess river called *amoad'ne*. The river was noted to have never run out of fresh water but forbidden to anyone including the hunter to drink. As a hunter/warrior he was an excellent mask-man and could use only a bow and arrow, and sometimes just a spear to kill fearsome animals like the buffalo, the elephant, lions, tigers and many others all by himself and alone in the thick forest. A forest where all that one could hear was the roaring noise of the king of the jungle, the lion and sometimes too, thunderous footsteps of obese elephants echoing miles away but appearing frightful and close in the eardrums. Within the enclaves of the unconscious mind, the ground appears to be swaying anytime these elephants fight.

Deep inside the forest and most often, especially during the day, whizzing sounds of different trees were heard and at night the wind uncontrollably whooshed, sounding very pleasant to the ears. Sometimes however, the red hunter will just enjoy the sweet and beautiful songs from the birds as he walks in and around making friendly but cautious advances towards reptiles and other animals. At weeknights, especially when the moon zoom it light to brighten that part of the world, he would simply retire under a big tree close to the river and count the stars. On one weeknight, he laid down blissed on a flat rock counting the stars as they appear on the sky together with the moon.

"One, two, three, four, five, six, seven," he counted. Inside the river, the frogs sang and danced to their song of a happy and beautiful home; a home forbidden to man and its activities. On that night, he just laid down listening to the songs from the frogs as he continued counting the little, little stars. Besides the songs of the amphibians, he could also hear welled coordinated melodies coming from other unknown living things which are usually unheard during the day and he continued to count till he could no longer see a star and went to sleep. He was the only one who could dare go to the river-side and come back home safely without the wrath of the gods.

"koo koro kooo." The cock crowed at dawn. *"koo koro kooo."* It shrilled for the second time and then the third time within sixty seconds but, it was the fourth one which came just fifteen minutes after the third crow that woke up the red hunter from his quiet sleep. The cock triumphs in a gloating tone. The red hunter knew all was well as he started to walk home with the six feet snake he had captured alive the previous day. The snake was still alive, and he wrapped it around his neck as he walked back home after many days of hunting in the forest. Usually, he likes to be away from the sight of the people, and this is why he is always on a hunting expedition. On his arrival in the village from hunting, most of the children who saw him that day with the snake immediately run to their mother's hut. Just a few brave ones among them stayed put to catch a glimpse of the snake which has its head erected up high and alive. Upon seeing him with the long snake, many of the village folks immediately suspected it was meant for spiritual enchantment since they knew him to be a mystical person.

He was born into a large ethnic group known as the Tarware in a town called Tiyaa-wumya. The Tarwares are known to be spiritually powerful and brave warriors as well. In his adolescent age he left his native home and moved to a nameless settlement where he dwelt for a short while and later moved to Zamfara. From Zamfara, he migrated to Malle on one of his hunting expeditions. While in Malle, he explored his hunting talent as well as engaged in farming activities for the rest of his life. He also fought and won many wars for the king of Malle and was therefore, giving the title *Toz na* (chief warrior). He married a beautiful princess, the daughter of the king. The black princess had seemingly good looks, dark in complexion, long bushy silky hair, dark eye brows, nice eye lashes, a pointed nose, and bright whitish teeth with some little space in the center dividing her upper molars appearing very beautiful whenever she laughs. Planted on both sides of her chest also, were two 'pear-shaped' breasts, fresh and soft. Her nipples were like a round juicy fruit. Although a lame lady, she had attractive hips and enough buttocks which tremble whenever she walks. These and the charming smiles always on her face caught the eyes of the red hunter.

His bravery and good hunting abilities also attracted the black princess and they both fell in love and got married. They begat a child a year later. A one-eye giant called Kpognumbu. He was still a baby when the black princess died and he grew without knowing her. His father also died when he was still very young.

CHAPTER TWO

H E WAS A stout hearted warrior and would have celebrated his 64th birth day at home with his family but for the war which he must go. It will be his sixth successful wars should he return home safely. The giant as he was affectionately called was known to be more revolting than his father. He also fought and won many wars and also migrated from one settlement to the other with his household looking for an uninhabited land to do farming and to settle as well. Unlike his father who had only one wife, he married many wives and had many children. His first wife gave birth to five children. The first two were twins, but they both died at infancy. The other three children, Namzi-sheli, Nyargili and Ngmalgensam however did survive. Sonyini, his second wife also had many children but it was only Gbewaa who survived. As the head of his household and in accordance with traditional norms, he called his only surviving wife and his eldest son to his room the night before he left for the war. His other three children were asked to remain seated in the dark room where all of them had assembled. He walked in and out of the room four times all alone holding a light. It was a piece of wood with fire and the brightness of it could not go beyond five meterstick.

On the fourth time that he walked into his room, he stood in the middle holding the light. Then, he looked directly into the faces of his two guests, Sonyini and Namzi-sheli. Down he went on his bended knees like a kneeling bus and stretched his hand towards his wooden bed where he pulled out a black clay pot from under it and gave it to his son. After giving the pot to him, he walked back to the isolated dark room where the other three children were seated. Few minutes later the two followed him there with the pot as instructed. But, as soon as they walked out and took a few steps forward to join them in the dark room, then, two mangos felt down from a tree in the middle of the house. One mango fell right in front of Sonyini, causing some fear in her and she quickly took a few calculated steps backward. The other one which was half ripe fell into the kraal where the animals had been lying down. The night was very quiet, dark and scary so they were both afraid being outside the room. Namzi-sheli pretended he wasn't afraid but the woman saw the fear in his face when she pointed the light at him. So, they both stood there with their legs very still and stiff.

"Take the lead. Aren't you the son of a warrior? What are you really afraid of?" She asked.

"But Mom, aren't you also the wife of a warrior? I know women don't run away from troubles even when men do. They stand and face it. Any way you can see that I'm holding the pot. Please take the lead Mom," he teasingly told her.

The back and forth notwithstanding, they finally joined him and the children in the dark room. She began to wonder what could be the reason for the summons. She therefore attempted asking the man why he has summoned all of them at this time of the night but, the looks in his face were terrifying enough to let her rethink; she quickly and wisely decided to remain mute but not forever. Then she noticed that the children were paying attention to the two of them so, she deliberately forced a loud sneezed just to distract them. She sneezed loudly and the vibration forced a little rat in the room to run out from its hiding.

"Why all this at this ungodly hour, my husband," she spoke silently to herself. "I surely will have to ask him this question at the right time," she added and simply swallowed her words and remain quiet.

The warrior continued to stare at her till she stopped looking at him and sat down. She sat close to the main door where she could see anyone coming into the house even though she knew that, at that time of the night, no neighbor will leave the comfort of his or her home and visit another neighbor. Perhaps, she just wanted to keep watch of her husband's horse. The white horse which was giving to him as a gift for his role in one of the wars he fought. The horse had been an object of envy in the village ever since it was given to her husband by the king.

Sonyini made an attempt to sneeze for the second time just to distract her husband from staring at her. But the man ogled her, and she stopped it immediately. She held on to her breath for about fifteen seconds and that aided her to stop the sneezing. The children then began to murmur when they saw their mother flirtatiously gazed at their father. They all seemed confused as well about everything that was happening in the room. But, the man knew what he was doing. Dressed in his unusual attire—a piece of white woven muslin cloth wrapped around his waist and in-between his two legs leaving only his broad hairy chest exposed, he stood there speechless but for a while. Then, he looked at the faces of the children as if something was missing in the house which he urgently needed to fish out the thief.

After staring at each of them one after the other, he finally instructed Namzi-sheli to place the earthen pot on the heaped sand at the extreme corner of the room where the wall was partly painted white. Then he pulled out from nowhere a tail, and said to him, "This is a lion's tail. It's the last lion your grandfather the red hunter killed many years ago before your mother was even born." He passed the tail over from his right hand to the left one holding it firmly and then brought out some skeletal remains of the pet snake Tohazie brought home. He then turned to all the children and told them the tail was given to him to symbolize the transfer of 'power'. To Sonyini he spoke softly to her, saying, "Take this piece of bone and use it to cook green *ayoyo* soup for the children."

He handed over the bone to her and whispered, "It's a snake. A female must not eat the soup if she wants to produce offspring or see her grandchildren. I'm aware I did not give you a female child. As you can see, all of them seated are males. You are the only female in the house and you must therefore not eat the soup or even taste it when cooking. It is a taboo for you to eat it and you know I also wouldn't mind if you add me more children." He then submerged the tail for about a minute into a preserved blood in the pot and brought it out. On the white wall, he made three short parallel marks with the wet blood. His guests just kept watching and confused as he drew the lines on the wall. They sat in total silence and watch till all the lines on the wall got dried then he began to speak to them.

"Sonyini,", he said, "as you may be aware, I will be leading the people of Boku in a war, tomorrow. I and my colleague warriors will have to leave this village before the rise of the morning sun. I have therefore scheduled to leave the house before the first cock crows. It's a war which I must go, because the king has asked me to." He winked his right eye as if he was communicating with one of them, but none of the children noticed it. Then he continued to talk, "I just got the message yester night from the palace messenger when you were still in your hut cooking," he said to her.

"I believe his footmarks could still be seen on the sand if you walk out right now. You see," he cleared his throat and continued, "The king's father was a very good friend to my father, Tohazie. My father fought for his father anytime there was a war, and as my father did, so shall I also fight for him whenever he needs me for a war and so also shall all of you do." He told the children. They all listened carefully and were very quiet as he spoke. "Now," he walked closer to the wall and said to them, "I want all of you to look at the wall where I drew the three lines in red. The red lines on the white wall are the blood of a leopard. The first line is for my father's father. The middle line is for my father, and the third one is for me. Again, I want you all to keep monitoring these lines as I leave for the war. I don't know when I'll be back but if you see the third line beginning to bleed on the wall, that means I will not come back home. On the other hand, if it does not bleed but turns brown like the color of a lion, then I will come back home."

He left all of them in the dark room and went out after he had finished telling them about the three lines. He didn't go back to his room. He just walked straight to the kraal and stood there for about two minutes and then moved to the hen coop where a bunch of multi colored doves descended and circled him and the coop. He went down on his knees and brought out three large white eggs from the coop and walked back to join his family in the dark room. In the room he placed the eggs on the heaped sand close to the dark pot and said, "This is why I called all of you here tonight. Keep watching the lines. You may now all go and sleep, goodnight." He concluded and walked back to his room holding the pot.

The woman followed him to his room still speechless and the children sat there motionless too and wandering. There was nothing they could do than to hope that the warrior will come back home alive and unhurt. Hope was their strength and one of the many things that all of them seemed to understand; they understood that in life the very last minute you lose hope that is the very last minute you lose what you hoped for. The children also went back to their room looking at each other faces as if that was where to find hope. Certainly, they couldn't have seen it in their eyes even if that was the only place to find it. Somehow, Namzi-sheli was the only one who didn't allow the fear of death overshadows his hope that his father will surely come home after the war. They continue to ponder fruitlessly as they lay down on their mats and the blood still on the wall dried. It wasn't bleeding as yet nonetheless the warrior was long gone. He left the house early enough not to be seen by anyone, not even Sonyini whom he passed the night with in her room saw him go. Hours later, after the cock had crowed for the third consecutive time, the children woke up and saw their mother sitting by boiling water on the fire.

One after the other they all walked passed and went out without saying anything to her, not even the proverbial morning greetings. They went out to wash their faces so that they could start the daily household activities. Nyargile was about to wash his face when it suddenly occurred to him to go and see if his father had already left for the war. With some speed he run back into the house and sharply greeted his mother and then headed into the warrior's room. He later came out looking sad and he said to the woman, "Mom, so father is gone and perhaps, never to return."

He then sat down next to the woman and close to the fire just watching the water boiling. He looked up into the sky then at Sonyini's face and the hope that they all had yester night was immediately renewed in him.

"Father will return safely." He spoke to his mother who was attentively listening to all that he was telling her. "Yes, father is gone; gone till the war is over and he will surely come back. I know he will surely return soon in his war regalia after the war is over. He will come with a human head in his hands and not a tail of a lion or a tiger or a snake but the head of a man." It was all just hope. Hoping and believing that no one can kill his father in a war.

"Never in a war before this one that he has ever been hurt and certainly not in this war either will he be killed or indeed in any war that he will go in the future." The woman was also very certain that her husband will come back home alive. She knew him very well and more than anyone else, and she knew he will come home. She turned and looked at the little boy with a sharp and soft smiled and tenderly gave him a pat on his head.

"You have spoken like a man, my son. The warrior will be proud of you."

"Thank you mother," he replied and then walked to the kraal. He was the first person to get inside the kraal that early morning even though it was not his turn to take the animals out for pasture, but he chose to do it that day. As was always with him, he seemed to have a hidden agenda. His kind gesture was therefore with question marks, but his brothers could not figure that out. In the kraal, he looked to his right, but it was not there. Then he turned to the left and began to search for it. The wild castrated ram saw him knelt down to pick the mango that fell from the tree yesterday. The ram moved backward bleating. It stopped, then backward again and stopped. Then unexpectedly it ran forcefully at him to attack. Nyargile saw it coming fearlessly, so he quickly ran to the north end of the kraal leaving the mango. The ram followed him there forcing him to jump over the black lamb twice. The struggling in the kraal forced one of the ewes to unintentionally step on the ripe mango. He wisely retreated and drew himself closer to the gate.

"Gbewaa, where are you?" He called. "Will you please get me a rope, I mean the nylon rope to tie this bastard," he instructed with anger and pain in his voice. Gbewaa responded to the call. He responded very quickly like a distress signal and appeared with the rope in a matter of seconds.

"I think I have to teach this stubborn 'thing' a bitter lesson."

"What could be the matter Nyargile," Gbewaa asked as he joined him with the rope?

"I'm glad you are here. Did you get the rope?"

"Yes. Here is it."

"Alright, just wait at the gate and make sure it will not push you over and escape."

"Yes. But what is the matter with that sheep, brother?" He asked him for the second time.

"Don't be inquisitive. Just make sure the gate is firmly closed. Just do what I say." He instructed. Gbewaa obeyed and was right in front of the door to stop any animal from escaping. The ram bleated again, *m'beeer m'beeer m'beeer* and lifted its right foreleg about to hit the ground several times. Nyargile looked at the mango and his anger immediately multiplied. With the anger in him he courageously went in for the ram with the aim to put the rope around its neck and make it powerless. But to his surprise the ram was not aggressive and offensive anymore; the wether sheep just surrendered, and cautiously he got hold of its two horns and placed the rope on the neck. Meanwhile, as all that was happening in the kraal, the trinity blood was still dried on the wall.

CHAPTER THREE

ON THE THIRD day after the warrior had left, they all gathered in the dark room and none of the lines was bleeding as yet, maybe never at all to bleed. They were happy, perfectly happy that the third line was still dried. They did not just hope this time around that he will come home unhurt but they were also very optimistic of seeing him home alive. They didn't however know when.

The fourth day the lines seem wet but not bleeding. They saw it but no one uttered a word. Perhaps, that wasn't their expectation. Then came the fifth day and the blood became dried up again, bringing some smiles back on their faces and also invigorating their optimism of seeing him back home from the war. The sixth day however seemed a headache for the woman. She saw the third line began to bleed but just for a while and it stopped. Yet, that was enough to cause fear and panic among the children as they began to ask if indeed the warrior will come back home. The woman couldn't sleep on the night of that sixth day. She stayed awake into the seventh day.

It was flurry and cloudy throughout the day. At night, the moon vanished, and the little stars were nowhere to be seen again, and the whole village became numb and wind chilled and the children went to bed hours earlier than the usual time, leaving her alone.

On that day she came out from her room at an ungodly hour wandering about her husband and hoping to see him home. She remembered he had whispered to her the night before he left, he whispered to her that he will be coming home on the seventh day if the third line is not bleeding. She thought about it for a while and went back to her room. She came out later holding a light, the same piece of wood her husband had used the night before he left for the war. She walked with it to the dark room just to update herself on what was happening with the trinity blood. "Hmm! Thank God," she said, when she realized that none of the lines was bleeding; not even the first line or the second one. Nonetheless, she stood there till she was convinced that indeed all the lines were dried before she went back to her room. She was also happy the children ate the 'snake soup' as instructed by the warrior even, though none of them knew what was used to prepare the soup.

The days flew faster and faster like a tornado but not destructive as one. It was exactly a week now since Kpognumbu left the house unnoticed. On the eighth day, he came home in the middle of the night and went in as he left the house. Quietly he walked into the dark room holding a bag with two human heads inside it. He walked straight to where the dark pot was and placed the two heads on the heaped sand. Then he sat on the floor and said the following words, "*M'ba Tohazie, duan ti dea komaasiri n'yu kaduane . . .*" He invoked the spirit of his late father to wake up and drink some ice water and then go back to sleep. This, to him was necessary because he knew his late father might have been thirsty in the grave and would therefore need water to drink as it was a belief of the people that the dead also drinks water just like the living although they do not talk like the living does. He continued to invoke the spirit of his dead father "*. . . N'leb-yinni na lafiana. N'naa.*" I've come back home safely. Thank you," he said as he poured libation to his dead father and to all those before him who died in a war. After that he wiped off the trinity blood on the wall and went to his room.

In September of 1593, nine years after he came from his last war all his children had now grown into adulthood and were now married. Gbewaa, his younger's son, now 28, migrated southwards and settled at Sanga with his mother Sonyini where he instituted chieftaincy. His elder brothers, Namzi-sheli and Nyargile also left the village and went to other places separately. The warrior refused to move out from Boku, his present abode to resettle elsewhere with the children. He however, promised he will always be there in times of war if they needed him. He also allowed his wife to go with her son to their new place. Following the death of his mother, and unsatisfied with the prospects after a brief stay at Sanga, Gbewaa moved out with his children a year after, and settled permanently in a hamlet known as Pusig where he was warmly welcomed by the inhabitants there. The people of Pusig were kind and peaceful. His good works, bravery and great leadership skills while at Sanga had spread wide and known in all the other villages near and far including Pusig.

He founded the Mawus kingdom at Pusig and was known to be a great and wise king. His reign witnessed the beginning of the coming of the white man into that part of the country. Like his father, he also had many wives and children and among his many children were three warriors, Zirili, Kufugu and Tusugu. He led his people into unity and prosperity until his saddened death.

As the spiritual leader of his people, his death was full of mystery. The night before, his cherished son was murdered and a violent storm engulfed the entire kingdom. The next day was solemn and he took the black earthen pot which he inherited from his father, turned it upside down, placed it into his head and slowly rocked into the earth at night and was never seen again.

It was a lovely sunny day especially in the early hours of the morning. Then it became partly cloudy later in the day, giving a chance of showers mainly in the evening. It became breezy with lows and winds, twenty to thirty mph. Two days after, the sun began to orbit alongside with the moon at night. Occasionally, it'll spread its circumference wide in an attempt to overshadow the moon. Perhaps, just to depict its superiority over the moon.

The superiority of day over night and may be light over darkness. They both continued to orbit around and around and around. "This isn't why you were brought here." The moon queried. The conversation between the two celestial bodies went on for seven nights as they continue orbiting side by side in watch of planet earth and all that which is in it; the people, the animals, the trees, the sea and everything that was made by Him. They could see everything on earth and they saw the murderer; the man who killed Kufugu. They saw him wearing a face mask and they knew who he was, but, they chose to remained silent and continued moving. They also saw how the king disappeared.

On the eighth day everything changed. The weather changed and so the temperature also changed and was sufficiently cold throughout the day till after noon. During the day, the sun surfaced momentarily and disappeared and then appeared again at night, rendering the moon obscured and dimmed. Fear began to run through the veins of the village folks like blood. The elders instructed the drummer to summon the people. He sounded the big drum in front of the palace to make the announcement. The sound echoed very loud and clear and the youth understood what that meant and so everybody in the village immediately gathered at the palace that night to join the elders perform the rituals after which they will go round the entire village from one house to the other pleading for the sun to leave the moon alone. They will also march along the streets amidst drumming, singing and dancing. They will sorrowfully sing songs of praises to their ancestors, invoking the spirits of the dead to intervene. They will also plead to the sun to spare the moon for the sake of peace and mutual coexistence. They will sing, "*zom naa-wuni kazawun basi, zom naa-wuni kazawun basi . . .*" They will just sing as they move around from one place to the other.

Everything went wrong in the village ever since the disappearance of the king as well as the murder of prince Kufugu. The continual orbiting of the moon and the sun at the same time created fear in the people and so the Christian community prayed to the messiah for His mercies. So did the Muslims. They prayed for God's intervention. The traditionalists also invoked the spirits of the gods asking for forgiveness and pleading with them to have mercy on the land and the people. Not surprising to them, the scientific community explained that it was just an obscuration of the light of the sun by the intervention of the earth. They simply described it as a lunar eclipse and further explained how such events do occur. They discredited the belief by the traditional community, that it was the anger of the gods on the people that is why all this was happening in the land. They further explained that an eclipse is an anomaly that occurs when the sun, earth and the moon align in a way that one blocks another from sight. This coincidental event they say usually occurs on the planet only because of its unique position within the solar system.

"From the earth, the moon appears to be the exact same size as the sun. This is because, even though the sun is actually about four hundred times bigger than the moon, it is also about four hundred times farther away. However, most often than not when they happen to align, the moon appears to block out the sun. But this time it was the sun that blocked the moon," they explained. This vivid explanation notwithstanding, the traditionalists where still not convinced; they believed the 'Whiteman' was deceiving them as usual and so they were not ready to buy into that line of reasoning. As far as they are concern, it is the anger of the gods on the people and not that it is the moon which has blocked the light of the sun as explained.

"The gods have spoken but it is not for the ordinary man to comprehend their language," they believe, as they rebuked the claim by the scientific community concerning the eclipse. "*Yimba yelni. Ni science, boa-nya science de-ei-pazeri maa?* (Don't mind them. That science, what is science if not lies?") One of them queried.

"Hmm, you have spoken well, Bonzuu. May your years be increase, even though for the past twelfth months this is the first time you have said something wise and I can't help but agree with you on this." Nomo sneered. He uncovered his bald head as he took off his red hat, probably to allow some fresh air to blow over it.

"My worry really is that, the oracles must be consulted for a remedy but the priest is also helplessly down with unknown illness. Perhaps, the gods might have been angry with him too, who knows? I even think he ought to have foretold the king about the conspiracy to murder his son even before the crime was committed. If that had been done, I believe it could have aided in preventing the perpetrators from committing the act," he added.

"There is no air here so you had better cover that 'thing' you have exposed, thinking you have a beautiful head . . ." Bonzuu said to him. ". . . or you rather plant some hair there and let it grow like a forest. In any case," he paused and continued, "Are you accusing the priest of negligence? You better watch your words; watch your words I said. Be mindful of what comes out from your mouth if not the gods will strike you to death. How dare you accuse the priest when your allegation could even be baseless and untrue?" He admonished.

Two days after the eclipse had ended, the morning sun was visibly up in the sky in its fullest circumference appearing yellow from the east—round and big with faded purple colors around its edges. It was a beautiful sun; very beautiful and bold. By noon the colors disappeared and the sun began to beam making the day very bright and sunny again. The sky was also beautiful with tremendous white clouds, very large and hanging loose. Late in the afternoon the sun resized to a semi-circle in mid sky, reducing its rays and ready to set in westwards.

One after the other they all walked into the big room where Nomo and Bonzuu were already seated. Architecturally, the meeting hall was built round with locally made materials and strategically located at the main entrance of the large palace building. It was a big palace with about thirty-five households. The meeting hall has a twin passageway; one is located inside of the palace and the second door is located directly opposite to the inside one from the outside of the palace in addition to the main entrance door. The outside door was short and shaped like an inverted 'U', measuring about four feet five while the inside door is five feet ten.

According to customary practices of the Mawus, anyone passing through either of the doors must take off his hat or anything found on the head before entering the hall. They all did as they walked in, except one of them who did not. Dressed in his pride of the north, popularly known as *fugu* (smock), the tall bulky looking man didn't only forget to bend down well enough to fit through the height of the door, he also forgot to remove his hat before entering and, as soon as he pushed forward his head to get in, he hit the top bar with his forehead causing his hat to fall on the ground. Quickly, a guard appeared at the scene and took the hat from the ground. He immediately handed over to him a tiny piece of paper to pay five cedis fined to the traditional council for violating the rule. "For your information the new rule is that you must pay the fine before the start of the meeting if not you will be disqualified from attending the meeting and that could also attract additional fine." The guard told him.

None of the elders spoke to a by-passer as they walk to the palace. Not even when they were greeted. Customs and tradition does not permit that especially when a chief passes away; it is considered a violation of rule eight of the established palace rules. They could only talk among themselves as they walk to the palace but not to anyone. They all came and the hall was full. The death of Gbewaa was indeed a great shock and almost all of them susurrate over it as they sat patiently waiting for the old man, the clan head. By his status as the clan head, Yamyolya was the only one who could enter the meeting hall through both doors as and when he deemed it suitable. On this occasion, he came in through the inside door with his two subordinates. The low crisp whispering did not cease even when he walked in, and it was becoming a little bit noisy as they continue to rustle. The old man then decided to clear his throat loud and deliberate just to call them to order. But his dexterity didn't work. It could not stop the noise so he repeated it for the second time. Then the third time and everybody lowered his voice. Slowly the noise died off completely and the hall became as quiet as a cemetery in the midnight.

A young man then took a calabash full of cola-nuts around and everyone dipped his hands into it and picked whatever his fingers had grab. He is the only one permitted by the gods to share cola-nuts on such occasions because of his hunchback. First it was the old man who dipped his hand into the small calabash filled with cola-nuts and brought out a big one. With his left thumb, he broke the cola into two equal parts and gave one to the man seated next to his right hand side; he is second in the seniority chain.

"Our elders have said that, he who brings cola brings life." The old man said.

"You're right. It's also a sign of peace and unity." Another man added.

"No doubt about that," the old man concurred.

"I wish to thank you all for promptly responding to my call. As a matter of fact, I invited you all to join me chew these cola-nuts and find solutions to the calamity that has befallen us ever since the sudden death of our king happened. The practice of sharing cola-nuts before the start of a meeting like this has been with us for a very long time, our forefathers, and even those before them, and we must therefore also continue with it," he told them.

"I greet you all once again, my fellow elders."

"We greet you too, our wise elder."

"Wise men, wisdom as our elders say is not in one man's hut. It is also said that, a head without wisdom is just a big load on the shoulders of its owner. Obviously, we have all gathered here today for a reason. As you might all be aware by now, that, what we have experienced in this land, I mean the plague that has befallen us for the past few days as a result of the death of our king and the murder of his son, is indeed a curse. Right now, our chief priest whom we rely on in difficult times like this is also ill and something must be done to stave off the situation from getting out of hand or else . . . So, in a nut shell these are my reasons for summoning all of you here today; we are here to look into all that which had happened in this our land for the past ten days or so." He formally informed them about the mystical vanishing of the king. He told them about the sudden illness of the priest and also about the eclipse as well as the murder of Kufugu. In fact, he told them everything that had happened and described it as an abomination which has invoked the anger of the gods on the land.

"We must therefore not sleep on this matter till the gods are consulted and appeased, for if we failed to do what must be done, the gods will surely abandon us also. Just last night two people came to inform me that the murder is an 'in-house' one. According to them they saw the one who committed the act. The assailant, according to them is a member of the royal family." He revealed, and everybody was mute. The room was therefore perfectly quiet. They listened to him as if that was their first time of hearing about the calamity. Perhaps, it is because of how he spoke gently and softly that got them pay much attention to him as though it was a folktale.

"I could not just accept what I was told to be the truth neither was I prepared to dismiss the allegation for, our elders say there cannot be smoke without fire. So, as a matter of fact, since yesterday when I was told about this allegation I decided to zip my mouth so that I could spew it out today for all of you to hear," he concluded. They all seemed not to believe that a brother could murder his own brother; at least, if what they have been told was anything to go by.

"Why on earth will he do that? Look at the calamity that has befallen us all in this kingdom just because of one person's selfish hatred for another. What a sin? It's indeed an abomination and whosoever committed this crime must be banished from this land. We can't afford to have him in our midst," one of them suggested.

"I think we don't have to allow the murderer to continue to live among us after invoking this curse on us. It is really a curse and if he continues to stay in this land after spilling an innocent blood it could cause more wraths of the gods on this land. Whoever it is must therefore leave the land till he is found innocent and the gods pacified before he could be accepted back in our midst. That is how our forefathers did to murderers. It is a tradition and we must not deviate from that. It must be strictly adhered to. We have gotten enough of his calamity already," said Bonzuu. Murmuring resumed but for a while. The young man again brought more fresh cola-nuts and some *pito* (locally brewed beer). The *pito* and the cola were meant to stimulate and energize them to deliberate more into the night if necessary.

"I greet you all, wise men of our land."

"We greet you too, Nomo."

"Yes, it is true that an abomination has been committed in this our land and there is no doubt about that. Indeed, the murder of any member of this land is loathsome, more so, a member of the royal family and a prince for that matter." He spoke aggressively and exact, with a serious look all over his face as if he was fighting with all of them for compromising with the truth concerning the murder. But that surely was not the reason. He was just simply making a point with much passion and worry.

"Urgently, I think we need to do something," he added, and sat down.

"Wise one," Aniyam said as he got up to speak, "I greet you all. I would want to believe that the accusers in this case if I may say so, are yet to prove that indeed they saw the accused committing the crime or, that they have reasons to suspect so. I'm of the view that, instead of banishing the accused person since we now know who he is, I think the best thing will be to hand him over to the police since criminal matters ought not to be handled by us. He could prove his innocence there," he concluded.

The meeting went into late evening and into the night as they continued to deliberate unmindful of the time. Their desire and willingness to get answers and find solutions to the problems was urgent. They have to find the killer before they could proceed to do anything else. At about 8:00pm, they all became weary and so the *pito* proved to be useful for them; it gave them the needed boost to be able to stay for that long period of time. In his smock of many colors which he was always proud of, Bunchara got up to speak. He carefully repositions his hat and was now ready to talk. He has been mute for all that while. He only listened and he never drank his *pito* either. His calabash was still full to the brim, and he only sipped just a little of it when he was about to talk. But before then he only concentrated on chewing a long piece of stick just to keep the mouth fresh and clean till he was ready to speak. Minutes after minutes he will just use the chewing stick to brush his teeth slowly and carefully, up and down, then to the left and right sides of his jaws. Then he will finish it up cleaning the top of his tongue. Occasionally also, he will spit out the pieces of debris from the chewing stick. He looked at Yamyolya directly as he spoke and asked multiple questions even though it was meant for all of them.

"Fellow wise men, if I may ask, don't we have our own way of solving our problems? Were we not solving our problems before the colonial police came to being? Must we really allow the white man to tell us what or what not to do and how to solve our own problems? Wise one," he took few steps and went closer to Yamyolya then spoke softly as if a whisperer. He said, "You see, we must be mindful of the fact that both the deceased and the accused are princes of this land. One of them is the elder and the other one the younger brother. The white man, our colonial master certainly does not know how our traditional set up, customary and traditional laws and practices work here in this land. They have their own system which works perfect for them in their communities and country but it might not be good for us. So, we must therefore understand that we were handling our own problems before the white man came with his foreign policing system. Let us not forget for a minute that we had our own traditional policing before the white man came here."

He turned and looked at Bonzuu and asked, "Please tell me my brother, if what I have just said isn't true. My elders, why must we now say this matter must be handled by a foreigner; someone who is not from this land. Why?" he quizzed as he turned to face those seated in westward direction. He continued, "my elders, let us not forget that in the first place the white man came and deceived us to accepting his religion by making us believe that ours is full of evil. He deceived some of you with food and his used clothing. They even promise us salvation and the coming of the 'son' of God only if we follow their religion. Over my dead body if I am to follow the white man's religion. If I may ask another question, does that mean our forefathers who died, and those before them will not receive salvation?" He vehemently objected to the trial of the accused prince by using the white man's law as suggested by some of his colleagues. He continued to argue that the white man will slowly kill their system of adjudication just as he had killed their religion, the African traditional religion, if they allow 'him' to always intervene in their matters. He paused and sipped a little of the *pito* then he wiped his wet lips with his palm.

"Is it not the same white man who told us he came to trade with us but ended up colonizing us? My brothers, instead, I will suggest that the wrath of our ancestors be invoked on whoever is responsible for the murder of our prince especially when it is possible that his elder brother, the accused, could be innocent and also there might not be fairness if a fellow human being is to determine the allegation. This is how our forefathers handled such situation." He concluded.

One after the other they all made their submissions. They talked, they discussed, and they drank. Some echoed above their normal voices while others seized the opportunity to make provocative remarks and name calling of those they obviously were not in good terms with. They rained insults, insinuations and accused each other for past wrongs but Yamyolya remained calm. He wasn't really enthused with the conduct of his colleagues, but he tried to understand them since it is always like this anytime they met, no matter the issues at hand. All these notwithstanding, it was unanimously agreed that the accused should be taking to the city to face the white man's law and prove his innocence.

CHAPTER FOUR

It was in mid-February, few weeks before he was killed. The accused and his deceased brother were in the Baby's Inn bar for a rest after a tiring long journey from Bulkwere. Seated at the far end and opposite the main gate of the bar was an albino lady with some few dotted black spots on her face. She was beautiful.

Zirili walked to her and enquired, "Hi, can I join you here, beautiful daughter of Eve?" She said nothing to him. He followed it up with a sensational smile and took a few steps forward, this time very close to her. Then, an eye-to-eye contact between them toppled his smiles, and invoking some romance in the face. She noticed it and quickly took off her eyes from him. She remained mute and seemed to be concentrating on her drink and pretending she was unaware who was standing next to her.

"Well, don't be alarmed at all, okay! I mean no harm to you," he assured her but the lady never said anything. She only managed to give a little smile back just to avoid creating the wrong impression that she was the mean type of person. He motioned himself further towards her and tried positioning his hand on her shoulder.

"Anyway, my name is Zirili but you can call me Z. The young man over there is Kufugu, my younger brother," he said. She raised her head up, looked straight at Kufugu and they both nodded to each other like lizards. Zirili then sat down though uninvited and extracted three thirty picas long smokeless herbal cigars from the inside-pocket of his white *fugu*. He volunteered one cigar to the young lady and one to his younger brother, and he kept the third one for himself.

"These are quite mild and the smoke isn't at all unpleasant," he whispered to her. The lady accepted the cigar, examined it carefully like a seasoned smoker and then nodded her head in approval to all what her admirer said.

"Thank you," she said. She reluctantly pulled herself a little closer to him and whispered, "Will you please buy a bottle of beer for me?" With the snap of his fingers the waitress appeared and lighted the cigars for them. The two men looked at the waitress and then nodded their head thanking her.

"What may I offer you, lady and gentlemen?" She enquired

"Please a bottle of star bear for the star lady and two bottles of Guinness for the men." They laughed but the waitress just smiled.

"Ok. I will be back in a jiffy," she said and disappeared.

"That might be a sign for love," said the albino lady.

"Oh no, it's just the usual excellent customer service expected from a good waitress. I think so." Kufugu replied. "As a matter of fact this is the reason why we came to this bar," he added. Minutes later, the waitress appeared again with three bottles of beer as requested. She was in her early twenties and her voice was smooth and melodic. The lady took the star beer and pulled Zirili with her to an obscured corner outside the bar to thank him for the drink. He followed her like a pet. At the corner, she sipped a little of the beer from the bottle and gave it to Zirili.

"It's nice. How do you know that I like star beer?" She asked and then took back the bottle of beer from him.

"Please open your mouth." She held the neck of the bottle and poured some of the beer into his mouth. Then she began some erotic moves on him; some of the things she had picked from her profession in the city. First, she placed her hand around his neck and stretched his fourth finger into his ear like a cotton swab and it looked good to him. She slowly and gently rubs his head down to the chin with her long shinny pink colored finger nails and said to him, "Thank you for the drink." She continued to press her fingers softly and gently down through his afro hair.

"I'm ok. Please stop it," he demanded. The lady did not mind. She continued with her moves—she rubs her fingers into his ears. "Stop that, I'm okay!" He said, and laughed. She also laughed and continued. His younger brother could not wait any longer sitting there alone, so he went to the counter and joined the lady there. He engaged her in a brief chat; he explained to her that he was bored sitting alone like a zombie waiting for someone who was elsewhere having a good time.

"That's funny but interesting," she remarked and they both laughed.

"And what do you plan on doing now."

"Well, that's why I came to you."

"Oh I see. So you want me to keep you company?"

"If only you wouldn't mind."

"Ok. But next time come with your own girl to avoid any inconveniences," She teasingly said and they both laughed. They laughed at everything the other one said about Zirili and the city girl and he seemed happy because he preferred talking to the bar girl than sitting there alone waiting and not knowing how long it will take the lady just to say thank you to his brother for buying her a drink.

The young lady continued with her thank you erotic moves. She wiped his lips with her fingers, held his waist with one hand and pulled him close to her like a magnet. He seemed a little bit nervously excited and he liked it but he didn't like the venue.

"Please, there are people watching can't you see. Just stop it. Oh my God, how did I find myself in such a trapped." She refused and continued the foreplay. "Oh, my God, will you stop it, you daughter of Eve," He screamed but in a quiet tone and laughed at the same time. Then he coughed as he discharged out the inhaled tobacco smoke through his nostril, and walked away like an escapee.

CHAPTER FIVE

WHILE IN HIS cells, and under 24hr protective guide, Zirili recollected some of the last moments he had with his deceased brother at the Baby's Inn bar after their journey from Bulkwere. He remembered all the good times he had with the city girl too. Right now however, the three of them were no more together; the albino lady had gone back to the city two days before his arrest and he may never see her again. Kufugu too was now dead and cannot be reached either, even if he wanted to have a drink with him again. He was now all alone in the cells accused of killing his own brother. He thought about everything that had happened and anything that came to his mind. He also remembered the disappearance of his father, the struggle for supremacy between the sun and the moon, the priest and everything. He remembered the night Yamyolya called him and asked if he knew something about the death of his brother. After processing all that in his mind, he only shook his head and spoke to himself, "Where did I go wrong or what at all have I done wrong?"

He got up and walked to the other side of the room furtively looking through a small window with his one eye as if he was looking inside a bottle. He wanted to see clearly what was going on outside but, he could not see anything except a shadow; not his shadow but the shadow of another man, the guard; tall and huge but looking short and fat in his shadow. The accused knew all the guards in the palace but he could not tell which of them was on duty just by looking at the shadow. He therefore motioned himself backward, away from the window and leaned onto the door on the opposite side just thinking; thinking about how to escape. Maybe so and maybe he was just thinking about his late father. The death of his father was still very fresh in his mind and so he continued to think. He could not also stop imagining seeing himself standing trial in the city court; all alone to prove his innocence even though he knew he did not kill his brother.

The third day after his arrest, the weather was dried and Pusig became hot and dusty. The people were still mourning the death of the king and the prince as well. Life was now gloomy to him. In the morning of that Wednesday the colonial police came with an arrest warrant to take him to the city after the elders had agreed to hand him over for further investigation and prosecution by the police.

"Mr. Zirili, we have a warrant for your arrest. You are therefore under arrest for the crime of murder. You have the right to remain silent. Anything you say may be used against you in court of law. The State will provide you legal aid if need be. You also have the right to a legal representative of your own if you so wish." The policeman read his rights to him and he chose to remain silent. The two policemen then handcuffed him into the police jeep and drove to the city where he is expected to stand trial.

Despite all the unfavorable weather conditions, the calamity and the death of the king, the rainy season began well the following month and farming activities could not be put aside like any other activity because farming was the only activity for their livelihood. Kombugus went to the farm two days after the first rain of the season to clear his farmland. It was indeed a reasonable downpour and the ground was muddy. He could not therefore ride on his 'metal horse' after a hard working day on the farm so he walked. He carefully walked on the two kilometers path pushing his bicycle till he got to the T-junction where he could safely ride the bicycle.

At the junction, he tilted the bicycle to his left side and carefully stretched his right leg over and above the seat and comfortably sat on it. Next, he placed his right foot on the pedal and using the left leg to stay stable on the ground. Then he sounded the bell, "*klin-klin, klin-klin*" signaling his readiness to be on the go. He knew there was not any creature on the road but somehow he just wanted to make sure there was not any ghost either. "*Klin-klin . . .*" he sounded the bell again and, off he began to ride home. Few hours after he had left the farm the sun was fully out at noon and the day began to look warm, beautiful and quiet. He got home with smiles dotted all over his face. His wife noticed it and understood what that meant; she knew he had a good day even though he looked calmly depleted as he got down from the bicycle. She had finished preparing *Tuwon-Zafi* (a meal made from maize or millet flour) before the fall of noon so food was ready for him to replenish the lost energy.

"Is the water ready?" She enquired from her son whom she had instructed to place a bucket of water in the bathroom for his father to bath.

"Yes, mom," Bakutoma replied.

The man went to the bathroom with a piece of cloth wrapped around his waist stretching downwards and a few inches beyond his knees, leaving only his bare hairy chest exposed. He was looking muscular. After he had finished taken his bath, he went for a rest under his summer hut and sat comfortably on the 'lazy chair'. He then turned on the radio to listen to music as he sat down just to keep his mind relaxed. The wooden box radio labeled made in England was hanging on a six inches nail on top of the central bar holding the summer hut. He seemed to like the song playing, so he slowly turned the knob of the radio clockwise to increase the volume, making it loud and clear. It was a traditional song of the Mawus; praising the achievements of each of the fourteen chiefs. Surely he was enjoying the music so much so that he did not bothered how long it will take to get his food served—it was one of his favorite songs with the chorus, ". . . *damba wariba ya wama katikuli, damba wariba ya wama katikul. Nabisi ya wama katikuli, damba wariba yawama katikuli . . .*" (. . . damba dancers, dance and let's go home, damba dancers, dance and let's go home. Princes, dance and let's go home, damba dancers, dance and let's go home . . .) this was what stirs his emotions so much making him feels proud. He sang along till the line died off slowly ending the song.

Bakutoma came out from the house holding a small table and placed it right in front of his father. He runs back to the house looking happy for no reason. Then few minutes later Mbangiba appeared from the house carrying a tray with two bowls and a cup of water in it. In the small bowl was soup and, *tuwon-zafi* in the big one. Still looking happy, Bakutoma followed her also holding a stool. The woman placed the tray on the table and knelt down to inform the man that food was ready.

"This is your food my husband. It is from the money you gave me and today I have cooked your favorite food. I know you are hungry after a hard day on the farm, please enjoy my food and make me happy." She said and smiled at him. The man pretended to be busy trying hard to change the meter band of the radio after the song ended, and the woman was still on her knees waiting for a respond from him before she could stand–up as tradition demands. After pretentiously struggling to change the radio station, he finally turned to the woman and nodded his head twice in acceptance to eat the food and also as an approval for her to get up from kneeling. He added a smile and thanked her for being a wonderful wife. Mbangiba then got up and sat on the stool her son brought. She sat close to his right hand side just to watch the man eat her food. He usually likes to have her around whenever he is eating. Perhaps, her presence stimulates him to eat better and enjoy her food the more.

"Aren't you eating with me, my wife?" He asked.

"I've eating already my husband. I prepared this particular food special for you because I don't want you to complain about lack of energy tonight," she said and they both laughed. He took a sharp pause from eating and gazed at her.

"Oh no," she said. "Will you please stop looking at me like that?"

"Is it a bad thing to look at your beautiful face, young lady? The face I've always loved to see even when I'm asleep. Mbangiba, as a matter of fact you look so pretty, please allow me to look at you as many times as I wish. Okay! In fact, I must add that looking at your beautiful face nourishes my eyes." He gave a deserving compliment to his wife and she honestly felt loved and happy; a feeling of renewed satisfaction of a good wife in the hands of a hardworking, responsible, loving and romantic husband. She smiled at him and said, "Thank you my husband. I must also let you know that anytime you look at me that way I feel loved and it reminds me of the first time we met. From that time on till today, I have never regretted marrying you. I knew you were a caring man, that was why I didn't refuse to marry you which was even against the wish of my father who was very much concerned about your tribe. He wanted me to marry one of the wealthy men from my tribe but, I insisted I was in love with a Mawus prince."

"Awe, so you still remember all that?" he asked and they laughed cheerfully but she said nothing about the question. He ate, and they spoke. The frequency modulation station had closed so there was no music playing any longer. After eating, he stood up and switched off the radio and then reluctantly sat on his lazy chair again. This time with all the weight he had gained from the food.

"Anyway, let me get in and finish with the daily housework before night falls," she said and went back to the house with the tray.

CHAPTER SIX

IT WAS A Monday, a fortnight after he was brought to the city. The morning was nippy but just for a short while. The courtroom was hushed and fully packed to its capacity that early Monday morning. All the seats were occupied and the old lady who had journeyed from the village to the city to witness the trial of the prince had no choice than to keep standing. Atipoka stood there for a while and then gave-up standing when she began to feel some pains in her knee joints. She therefore quietly walked alone to a distance tree with the aid of her walking-stick. Under the tree she took off her pair of *kala-belwala* (sandals made from warned out car tires) and carefully sat on the ground. Meanwhile court proceedings were ongoing but not connected to the alleged murder case involving Zirili. It was not to be his turn to take the accused dock till after the fifth case is over before the clerk will call his case. The two accused persons for the second and forth cases standing trial for stealing were at large; they had jumped bail and so a bench warrant was issued for their arrest.

"Case No. 172/75, the State versus Zirili." The clerk called and the accused calmly walked to the wooden dock under a police guide. He entered the dock with a focus eye contact on the judge and sometimes, a quick one at Bachela, his lead attorney. His lawyer was fully armed with law books ready to quote the Whiteman's laws and also make references to similar cases that had happened many, many years ago where the accused was acquitted and discharged. After a short rest under the tree Atipoka came back to accomplish her mission when she heard the name of the accused being mentioned—she came to witness Zirili's trial and nothing more than that.

The judge took a sharp glance at the stainless-steel clock hanging on the wall and it was, 3:45pm. He noticed that the sun had just begun descending slowly in the sky towards the west. The clerk who was smartly dressed in his usual attire—a pair of black trousers, a white long sleeve shirt and a black overcoat and tie to match, carefully read the charge sheet word by word just to make sure he never misses even a comma or a full stop as typed by the stenographer. He read the typed words on the paper and where he needed to pause because of a comma he did, till he got to a full stop.

"Prince Zirili Gbewaa," the clerk called his full name and read the following words to him, "For that you on February 17th this year at about 2:16pm, at Natinga, a suburb of Pusig and within the jurisdiction of this court . . ." The 'standard-seven' British trained colonial court clerk tried to showcase the little 'Queen's language' he had learnt from his British teacher as he read the charge sheet. Interestingly though, as much as he tried to sound like a British, the more he confused the man standing in the dock as he tries to pronounce the words. The crowd was also a problem for the accused; very intimidating so Bachela walked to him and whispered, "It's no problem. We have many interested people who come to court and this place, as you can see, attracts a number of intriguing men and women so don't panic at all about the crowd, okay!" He said as he tried to calm the nervousness of his client when he realized that the crowd was posing a problem for him.

"Is prosecution ready to start this case today?"

"No. Your honor, in view of some new developments we will only present the facts today and request for a date for omnibus hearing."

"How about counsel, do you have anything to say to that?"

"No, my lord."

The prosecutor then read the facts of the case as follows. "My lord, the facts of the case before you are that, the accused in this case and the deceased are brothers. They are both children of the late king, Na Gbewaa. Your honor, sometime in February this year, precisely on the 17 day between the hours of 10:00a.m and 2:00p.m, the deceased was in the house of the accused in the company of his friend. Your honor, at about 2:30pm, the deceased and his friend left the house of the accused after dining with him. Investigation conducted so far revealed that on their way home, minutes after the deceased and his friend left the house of the accused he complained of severe stomach pains and dizziness. Nyelba, his friend, immediately drove him to the Presbyterian Hospital where he was admitted. Unfortunately, my lord, the deceased passed away in the hospital that very day in the late hours of the night, and his body has since been brought for autopsy here in the city hospital. We are currently waiting for a pathologist report on the cause of death. Your honor, preliminary investigation conducted by the police necessitated the arrest of the accused. I must however add that before he was brought to the city to stand trial, the local traditional elders, I mean the council of elders of the royal family arrested and detained him based on a tip off. The matter was then reported to the police, and the accused was subsequently arrested and brought to the city for further investigation. These are the facts of the case your honor," he concluded.

The diminutive prosecutor presented the facts and he seemed satisfied. At least, it was visible in his face; his facial expression was full of smiles as he sat down looking at the defense attorney. He knew Bachela long ago when they were both studying Criminal Justice at the Law School. It was his turn so Bachela stood up to speak for his client. Reluctantly, he placed his left hand inside his pocket as if he wanted to pull out something magical. The weather was windy and so his long blue tie was swaying around and sometimes over and above his shoulder involuntarily. He carefully repositioned the tie on his small protruding stomach containing fat. In one of his several appearances on a different case, one of his colleagues mocked him by suggesting that he should consider being a friend of the gym as well and not only the court.

"Your honor," he said, "I must say that I am yet to have briefing on this matter from my client. As a matter of fact, I just had his instructions this morning to enter appearance for him. However, that notwithstanding and considering the fact that the accused has been in police custody for over the mandatory time limit and more so his arrest and detention was based on a misleading suspicion that, he killed his brother. I am therefore humbly applying for bail, but I am okay with a date for omnibus hearing, your honor." He spoke with maximum confidence, believing that he will get his client released on bail.

"My lord, investigation on this case is ongoing and the prosecution prays the accused will be remanded in police custody for some time. As a matter of fact after pre-evaluation of the evidence gathered so far, it is clear that we could have more substantial evidence to implicate him if we are given more time to complete the investigations. We have therefore set in motion a broad investigation into the case and will not want him to impede on our unfinished investigation. On that premise I pray my lord will remand him to police custody to enable us have a smooth investigation. Thank you, my lord." Prosecution's submission for no bail quickly brought defense counsel to his feet again. The accused was timid as he began to sweat inwardly when he heard the prosecution requesting for his further detention. He looked at the prosecutor with a genuine worry and anger. Bachela questioned the bases for no bail and reminded the judge that the arrest of his client was also unnecessary in the first place if not unlawful on the part of the royal elders.

"Your honor, in the first place, if indeed prosecution lead witnesses have not been to the police to give their statements why was the accused arrested, detained for more than a week by the traditional authorities and later by the police? On what bases at all, your honor was he arrested? These are fundamental issues of abuse of authority on the part of the elders, who took the law into their own hands without recourse to the fundamental rights of my client. Well . . . This case has been in the hands of the police for a reasonable time and they have the ability to have done an in-depth investigation before even arranging him for trial. But, what happened instead, they never bothered, but rather saw it necessary to cause an immediate arrest and rushed him to court. Again, there is no doubt whatsoever in my mind that the accused would not even attempt to abscond or be an impediment to investigation."

He paused and sipped a little water then continued "My lord, I must say that the accused is the elder son of the late king whom we all revered, he is a respectable person and principally the heir apparent to the throne and as tradition and custom demands, he must be present to perform the funeral of his late father. He is a conservative when it comes to tradition and he understands fully well what will happen to him if he fails to be at his late father's funeral as well as his late younger brother, the deceased in this case. So, it beats my imagination, the argument that he may abscond, or will be a hindrance to police investigation on this matter. In any case, why will he impede investigations? I believe there is no one in the kingdom, more disturbed and concerned about the death of his brother and father than the accused. I must say that as a matter of fact it really amazes me, the reasons prosecution is advancing in support of no bail. My lord, the accused is an honorable and responsible family man and will not be an impediment on the way of the police in this case. I must also add that he has some of his properties in the city and will always be available if needed by the police." Bachela paused for a while, and then took a few steps towards his client in the dock. He looked at him as if he was going to pull out the truth from his innocent face. He walked back towards the witness dock as he continued to advance his argument for bail.

"Your honor, what is more surprising and worrying to me is the fact that it is rather the accusers of my client who have failed to avail themselves to the police for a successful investigation. To me, and I believe my lord will agree with me on this as well, that, this somehow surely creates reasonable doubts as to whether this innocent man did indeed kill his brother. At the right time we will prove to the court that he never killed his brother. Honestly, I am tempted to believe that either the prosecution is not interested in prosecuting this case; most probably because they do not have the evidence to support this frivolous charge or that, they just take delight in detaining him for other reasons than the reasons adduced so far. The accused before you, your honor, is a decent noble gentleman who is a law abiding citizen. I'm therefore assuring the court that he will not be an obstacle in the way of the police in their effort to unravel the mystery surrounding the death of his dear brother. As a matter of fact, we believe that if indeed thorough investigations are carried out objectively and fairly well on this matter that is, if my lord decides not to discharge him for want of prosecution it will rather be in our favor but I pray my lord will dismiss this case." At this point, Bachela turned and looked straight at the bulky face of the judge and his focal precision was on his eyes then he spoke directly to him in a low tone.

"Your honor, it is also my sincere hope therefore that you will turn down the request of no bail as put forward by the prosecution and grant the accused a deserving bail. Thank you." He reiterated his desire to see his client on bail. The trial judge listened to both submissions carefully in their presentation. In deciding, he considered among other reasons, the fact that as the heir apparent of the kingdom it will be unwise for the accused to jump bail if granted. That notwithstanding, his overriding consideration was based on the fact that the alleged crime committed by the accused was a first degree felony and very sensitive; attracting the attention of everybody including the colonial Governor.

"This court have taken into accounts all of the necessary points raised on this issue and have conclusively decided not to grant the accused bail. This case is therefore, adjourned till Mach 23rd for hearing. I must however, add that, if the prosecution fails to finish its investigation by next court sitting, I will not hesitate to grant the accused bail." The Judge spoke softly with a very relaxed facial appearance but with some authority in his voice. Bachela was standing with his mouth agape in disappointment as the judge read his decision on whether to grant or not to grant bail to the accused. He only watched his client go with the police in handcuffs.

CHAPTER SEVEN

THE DAY WAS still young and in the sky the white clouds were evenly spread and bright. There was no bird flying and so the sky was just empty and quiet. The weather was generally good; a little warm and airy. The noise from the rice mill adjacent to the police station woke the detective up from his unintended nap. He took a sharp look at the clock on the wall. The time was fifteen minutes past ten. Through the window, he stretched his neck out to see outside. He was not looking for someone it just prompted on him do look outside, and he did.

"What!" He exclaimed; he knew it was too early for him to be sleeping, more so in the office.

"We ought to have been there an hour earlier. Oh no, I only hope she will be in the house. I just can't believe that I was sleeping at this early hour of the day." Quickly but gently he wiped his face with his soft palm then he removed the built up goopy from his eyes with his finger. Detective sergeant Wintima, known by the local community as 'Salmanja', turned to Lindsay who was busily reading the daily newspaper and asked, "Can you believe that?"

"Just listen to this, my brother. I woke up this morning and breakfast was ready, waiting for me. When I got to the dining table, I realized that it was a warmed left over of my favorite *Tuon Zafi* which I couldn't finish eating last night. I told my wife I didn't want to eat anything heavy this early morning, especially not when the weather looks good and can easily tempt one to be dull and lazy during the day. All I wanted was just a cup of hausa kooko (local pourage) with koose (beans cake) from the old lady who sells it just across the street and I would be ok but she insisted I must eat her food. That is funny. Don't you think so?" He asked and was expecting him to say yes or no but Lindsay never uttered a word. Then he continued after a brief pause.

"Guess what's interesting; she even promised to give me the money. I guess you know what I'm talking about?" Lindsay was still mute. He only looked at him, smiled softly and then flipped the newspaper to another page and then laughed and continued to read the paper.

"I remember when I made the request the other time she categorically told me she had no money. Can you imagine that?" Salmanja asked again.

"And so you ate the food?"

"Well, yes I did."

"And you accepted the money too?"

"Yes of course I did even though I initially managed to pretend I didn't need the money again. I think she didn't realize that I was only pretending so she continued to assure me that she will give me the money. Funny! Isn't it? Well, as you also would've done, I ate the food."

Lindsay stopped reading the newspaper and began to laugh very loud and so annoying.

"What's so funny about this that makes you want to laugh your head off?" He asked him and sounding displeased.

"Oh no, it isn't anything really funny. Just that it's amazing what your wife is prepared to do for you because of breakfast and maybe, it might really look funny that you also ate the food. But anyway, why didn't you refuse to accept the money?"

He laughed again and then refocused his mind back on reading the newspaper. It was an article concerning a possible 'conflict' and division looming among the children of the late king. In the article, the writer rumored that the children might even move away from Pusig to settle in other places.

"My wife is just a wonderful lady and I'm happy to have married her. Indeed, I'm proud I'm a married man," Salmaja playfully mocked. Lindsay heard him clearly but he completely avoided any contributive comment that could spark a long debate between a married man and a single man. He just did not want to subject himself to any discussion on marital issues that could give him stress. Minutes later he got up and walked to the next office where he could see the woman selling the roasted plantain. From the inside of the office he looked through the window and saw a long queue waiting. The queue was long enough to block his view from seeing the main charge office where a crowd had gathered like clouds. He couldn't see the woman who was selling the plantain.

Lindsay went back to the office and sat there for a few minutes. Then together with Salmaja and Lisa they left for the accused house and exactly at 12:30pm they got to the house. Lisa pressed the door-bell and it rang, "ding-dong!" ding-dong!! No one answered. She pressed the bell again and it rang for the third time, ding-dong. Then it rang again for the fourth time.

"Hello, who is there? A lady answered and quickly walked to the door.

"Good day!" she greeted and then asked, "How may I help you lady and gentlemen."

"Well, we are from the Police Head Quarters, criminal investigation division C.I.D and . . ."

"Oh I see, come on in. I have been expecting you about two hours ago."

The investigators followed her in and they could see that Sugru was truly an unhappy person but she tried to make them see the opposite side of her that truly defines who she is. She was able to show them her usual pleasant smiles and her eyes look happy though she was sad and the detectives detected it as soon as she showed her face when she open the door to let them in.

"I'm detective Sergeant Wintima."

"Lisa is my name."

"And I'm Lindsay . . ."

The three officers pulled out their service IDs and showed it to her after introducing themselves.

"We sincerely apologize for not coming on time as scheduled. Please accept our apology."—Lindsay.

"Never mind officer, I guess you were busy handling other matters as well. Am I right?"

"Yes, that is right, madam." Salmanja answered and smiled. "We're told the late prince and your husband were very good brothers." He added.

"That is correct. Thank you, officer. Please sit down and make yourself comfortable."

"No thank you madam but we truly appreciate your kindness. As you are very much aware, we're here in connection with the death of your brother-in-law and we would like to ask you some few questions, please."

"Please sit down officers." She insisted. They sat down curiously looking around the living room. They seemed to like the beauty of the house. It was a three-floors building. One of the few privately owned modern buildings in the heart of the city.

The house comprises of five bedrooms, two large living rooms; one on the third floor and the other on the second floor. It also has a mini bar, an office, and a multi-purpose kitchen all located on the first floor. It has a garage attached to the basement as well, and the natural scenery around the house was striking. The officers wished they could own such a magnificent house. It was just a wishful thought. They knew it could take them a life time savings to even get a parcel of land to buy in the city, let alone building such a house. They could only imagine the great deal, hard work and determination it took the accused before he got his dream house in the city. The woman excused herself and went to the kitchen where she was cooking.

"I believe this is one of the few mansions we have in the city." Lisa whispered. She couldn't hide her thoughts about the house after the curiosity. In the kitchen Sugru turned the knob of the burner and lowered the fire. She then came back to the living room holding a tray with drinks and water.

"Please these are for you. I guess you're all thirsty," she said.

"No thanks madam but we really appreciate your kind gesture."

After they had all sat down for a while and acquainted themselves, Lisa began to question her. "Mrs., if I may ask, where was your husband in the early hours of February 17?" She asked.

"Well," she said, "my husband and I were together with the children in the house. We were in the village on that fateful day. I do remember it was a Saturday."

"Okay. Can you tell us what he was doing in the village since he is most of the time here, in the city? We learned that at least for the past two years he has spent most of the time here in the city."

"It was one of our annual visits to the village to see the family back home and also to spend some time with his father, friends and love ones."

She continued, "At the village, my husband told me he was going to visit his younger brother the deceased, who apparently was also in the village that week.

"Madam, can you tell us what time he left the house?" Wintima asked.

"I'm not quite sure of the exact time but I think it was half past eight. Something like that. Yeah. I think so."

"Was it *Am* or *Pm*?"

"It was in the morning," she answered. "I remember he told me that the king had asked them to go to Bulkwere and take care of some pertinent matters concerning the community."

She answered all the questions and told them everything she could remember that had happened during their one week stay in the village. She was brief and straight. Lindsay didn't ask a question. He only took notes of the questions and answers. After spending about an hour at the residence of the accused, they left with an elusive dream—a dream of owning such a mansion one day in their life. But most importantly they left the house with the understanding that they need to do a thorough investigation on the matter if the State is to win the case. They understood that the defense legal team would put up its best on this matter, and they knew how excellent Bachela is when it comes to legal issues.

CHAPTER EIGHT

BAFA GROUP OF Attorneys is a law firm that commands a lot of respect in the legal circle and Bachela is considered one of the few outstanding lawyers in the country who often pursued cases to their logical conclusions. He is noted to have won almost all of his cases most of the time. He also encourages matters that could be settled outside the dictates of the law if possible, and handles them to the satisfaction of all parties involved. He is a lawyer of national and international repute; the first from Zotinga to have been trained in the USA as a Barrister and Solicitor at Law. His brief stay in the UK also afforded him the opportunity to learn the 'Queen's language,' making him very suitable as a practicing lawyer in a British colony with British laws. He could speak the British English so well to the delight of everyone and the investigators are very much aware of that.

On the fifth day, four days after the police had been to the accused wife, the defense attorney also went there to see Sugru. He had had discussions with the accused the previous day in prison custody and was now ready to ask his wife a few relevant questions. He did the questioning and Sando carefully wrote down everything that has transpired between him and the woman. He made sure he wrote down all the questions and answers—everything that was asked and all the answers that were given. He didn't leave anything out because everything mattered.

"I hope there isn't any addition or subtraction of words."

"No sir," Sando answered. He wrinkled his forehead and smiled.

"Sir, I realized she was getting chafed at some of the questions especially when you asked if she knew something about the death of her brother-in-law."

"Wow! So you detected that too? I hope you did not write that down as well?" He teasingly asked, and they just laughed.

"You see, that is the nature of the job as you may know by now. As a lawyer, you need to know everything about a case from your client or anyone who could be a source of information in the case so as to enable you put a good and strong defense but they seem not to understand when we ask such questions."—Bachela.

"You are right sir. I also realized that she was not happy at all, especially when you asked her whether her husband stands to benefit from the death of his younger brother because it is believed that the late king liked Kufugu more than her husband."

"That was a great observation. I truly enjoy working with you, Sando. In fact, apart from you depicting some high level of knowledge in law you are also hard working. But hey, tell me, what do you know about 'Trust Agreement' (T.A) and how well do you know about 'Contracts' too?" He asked.

"Hmm, well, just what I learned from the school," he answered. "Plus what I picked from a few cases when I was clerking in the High court."

"Oh ok. I see. Well, I may assign you to handle a case on 'T.A' one of these days."

Although Sando had learned all this in the law school, Bachela still considered him as a green leaf; a learner, a beginner, a new known because he has not accumulated enough experience to earn the total confidence of a senior legal brain like his boss even though he still exhibited some good legal argument on serious cases. As an experienced lawyer, he knew that learning the law in the classroom is quite different from putting what you have learned into practice.

The two lawyers left the accused house and drove back to the office. He went straight into his office and came out later holding a green flat file which the secretary had placed on his desk.

"I will like to use this in court on Monday. It has been through the word processor. Could you please read and check everything down to the last comma?" He asked and handed over the file to him.

"You see, the law firm is a jealous mistress and most of us regrettably have little time for our families. As a matter of fact, a single man like you therefore, may prove a distinct advantage. Anyway, I hope you're planning to join our club soon, the couple club (C.C)" he enquired.

"The C.C is another interesting place that one can share, and learn about marriage and it challenges. Unlike the law, marriage, as I've come to understand it, is a life time school of study that has no certificate or diploma. It's not for those who want the honey or milk of it but, for those who see it as a blessing and understand the challenges that come with it and are prepared and ready to make it a blissful union. Trust me, at C.C we do some little gossiping too at times. Don't think it's only women who do that. Men do it too but, somehow we do it just for the fun of it." The two laughed and held hands and joked about it. Sando particularly liked the conversation especially how Bachela described the law profession as a "jealous mistress." He liked the part of the C.C too.

He accepted the assignment and took the typed documents to his office to read. Seemingly tired that day he sat on his desk, shook his head and said to himself, "this seems like a job for a clerk, indeed. Anyway . . ." He opened the file and brought out the stack of papers in it and started to read. He became very tired, and weak after going through the documents. Indeed, he had a long day, but he was not anxious to go home for a rest. He simply placed his head on the table for a nap.

"Is anything the matter? Are you alright, my brother? You aren't yet married, but the disease seemed to have caught up with you so soon. You seemed worried I must say."

"Hmm, well, then probably the notion that the law profession is a "jealous mistress" only to those lawyers like you who're married and that, the unmarried lawyer could prove useful may have to be revised. Sir, with my experience in my case, you see, though I'm not married, honestly I believe there is no any difference between me and a married lawyer. Could you believe that my fiancée is the type who complains that I'm married to my job and therefore, do not spend time with her? She said that the weekends aren't enough for her so she therefore, wants me to be with her all the time and always even when . . . Just imagine this and you may understand me. You see, with me, Fridays reminds me of a restless weekend to handle. Saturdays aren't rosy at all but, thank God, Sundays brings a sign of joy to my heart because I know the next day will be Monday and Monday through to Friday I will be working. I really love my work but my fiancée is a jealous mistress to my work, maybe more than your wife." Again, they laughed. They both seemed to have enjoyed the comradeship and the conversation so, they simply laughed over it. The two attorneys were just a perfect pair in the legal field, and they enjoy working together.

Dinner was ready, but none of the children seemed to have appetite for food. They all retired to bed earlier than usual. The house was therefore, very quiet that night—there was no any necessary noise; the usual blaring of radio and television noise and so a fall of a pin on the floor could even carry an echo. They just went to bed without eating but with the hope that the police will get to the bottom of the matter and possibly apprehend the culprit. Like her children, Sugru also hoped so. She however could not sleep, unlike the children. She just knelt down by her bedside that night and prayed for the children. She also prayed for her husband too and hoped he will be released soon when the truth is out. After she had prayed, she then lay down on the bed sleepless and began to ponder over everything; everything that matters to her including the question asked by defense attorney, "Whether her husband could benefit from the death of his brother." She also remembered that Lisa had asked her similar question the other time, and she hates to hear people making any such suggestive questioning or comments.

Saturday April 02 she went to the Police Station with Ngudi to see her husband. At the station, little Ngudi saw his father walking under police escort with handcuffs in his hands. "Daddy, Daddy!!" He shouted above his voice in excitement. He was happy to have seen his father. The accused heard a voice calling, and it seemed to come from a far distance; far away from him. He ignored it thinking it was just his own imagination. But he continued to hear the voice calling, "Daddy, Daddy, Daddy." Familiar with his son's voice, he was now convinced that it was real and near, he turned to see his son. The little boy waved at him and asked his mother where the policeman was taking his father to. He tried running to him, but Sugru pulled him back.

"That is my son," the accused told the constable and smiled at the little boy. He tried waving back, but he could not; the handcuffs will not allow that so, he only managed to raise both hands up high to the shoulder level and attempted a wave. He was a happy man at least; so happy to have seen Sugru and Ngudi. "Mama, where is daddy going?" he enquired again.

The woman stood there speechless while looking at her husband in handcuffs. She simply could not believe it. As she stood there motionless, a tear drop fell from her right eye, but the little boy did not notice that. The second drop came, and then it started to drip from her eyes. She tried to hide it so, she quickly wiped the tears off and pretending to be a happy mother as usual. She stood there looking at her husband being escorted through the crowded lobby by constable Azumah who had a spring of youthfulness in his steps as he walk through the crowded lobby with the accused. Azumah released the handcuffs off from his hands, and he felt a little relaxed and somehow free. He was happy to have his lawyer there with him so, he was very much at ease and comfortable to answer any question. The constable guided him to two vacant chairs place closed to each other in the C.I.D's office. He sat face-to-face with the investigator for his second interrogation since he was arrested.

"Have you ever been to the Baby's Inn Bar with your brother within the last few months?" The investigator asked.

"Yes sir. I have."

"And when was the last time you went there?"

"I think that was three months ago after our journey back home from Bulkere?"

"Ok, when did you make that journey to Bulkere?"

"I cannot remember the exact date?"

"Was it only the two of you who went there?"

"No."

"Right, can you tell the court who was there with you and the deceased?"

"Well, there were many people in the bar with us."

"Oh I see. But did you go with a lady there?"

"No," he answered. The accused was brief and short in his answers. He only provided detailed answers as and when allowed by his lawyer and the investigator was getting frustrated about that. He told the investigator what had transpired between him and the deceased that very day before his death. He told him it was on a weekend and that, on most of the time they do meet with their families for recreation anytime they were in the village. "I either visit him or he does, and this has been going on between us for a very long time now. On that day in question, my late brother called to tell me he was on his way to my house. Half an hour later he came, but this time without his family as it has always been." The accused further stated that as a matter of fact the deceased came not alone but in the company of a friend, and at that time he was about to have his bath but later decided to sit down with them for a while before taking the bath. He added that the two of them had already planned to travel to Bulkwere on that very day.

"After I had finished taking my bath the three of us left for horse riding and we came back late in the afternoon to eat; we were really tired and hungry, and apparently my wife had already prepared food by the time we got home. We ate the food together after which Kufugu and his friend left for home," he told the investigator.

"Did you ever travel with the deceased to Bulkwere. If yes, when?"

"Yes we did. Indeed, the two of us traveled to Bulkwere a day before the Saturday in question."

"So, who is this friend you're talking about?"

"I remember he came with one Nyelba, the firewood man."

The investigator got up from the chair and walked to another vacant chair at the far end. He sat on it just to reflex his muscles. After sitting for a while, he pulled the chair closer to the defense attorney as if he is to interrogate him too. Sando adjusted himself to his chair and drifted away towards his client. He whispered, "Well done. You have not implicated yourself in any way so far, and I can assure you that we will do our best to get you acquitted. Bachela will be in court on Monday, because of this case," he assured him.

The police never interrupted the lawyer. He only waited and watched him whispering to the accused. Few minutes later he came back to the accused and continued with the interrogation.

"Now, apart from the three of you, was there anyone else in the house that day?"

"Yes."

"And who was that person?" he asked as if he wasn't really interested in getting an answer from the accused. "My sister-in-law was with us."

"Who is she?"

"Laa-misi, but her friends call her Laam."

"Alright, thank you. I think that is all for now." Within a short period of time, the investigator had asked him several questions. He repeated most of the questions his colleagues had asked the other time. The interrogation went on smoothly because there wasn't the usual noise from the rice mill and so the station was serene; very suitable for interrogation. The accused told his story of innocence and was very accurate with his answers; exactly what he had told his lawyer the other time was what he told all the four different officers who interrogated him in one way or the other. There was no deviation from what he wrote in his caution statement either. The prosecution team seemed satisfied with its preliminary evidence gathered so far, which they intend to use for trial after the omnibus hearing. From the new evidences gathered, the team decided to jointly charge the accused, his wife and his sister-in-law for trial.

On Monday April 04 at 8:30am the courtroom was fully packed with all kinds of people interested in the case. The old woman again was there in attendance. The royal family was also fully represented by members of the council of elders led by Bunchera. The pressmen were there too. They sat in the front lane ready to take notes and report as news. They were just eager for any sensitive information from the royal family that could make good news headlines. At exactly 9:05am the trial Judge came in, and all was set for proceedings to commence.

"All rise!" The interpreter ordered, and the spectators rose up in compliance. Then, the clerk ushered in the judge. Wearing his usual attire of a black suit, a big black gown over it and a white wig on his head, he came in walking majestically and looking scary in the outfit. One after the other, the three accused persons, Zirili, Sugru and Laa-misi walked to the dock as the clerk called their names. They were all jointly charged for conspiracy to commit murder and, murder. Bachela and Sando were also seated, and ready to battle it out with the prosecution. The State prosecutor and the C.I.D man were also there calmly seated.

"Your honor," it was agreed during our last sitting, that we will have an omnibus hearing today. This I must say was at the request of the prosecution. I wish to inform your honor that, the State is ready for trial in this matter, instead. We also wish to apply to substitute the old charge sheet with a new one and also with two additional names as accused persons. The charges against all the three accused persons as indicated on the charge sheet will be the same, but we also intend to make amendments to the facts, your honor."

"Application granted. Counsel are you ready?"—Judge.

"Yes, your honor. However, this is a sharp U-turn on the part of prosecution and I am surprised they failed to communicate this latest development to us. Nonetheless, we are ever ready, and I am representing all the three accused persons in this case. Thank you,"—lawyer.

All were seated, and the courtroom was quiet as the clerk rose to read the charges to the accused persons. This time around he did not attempt to speak like a British. He only carefully read the charge statement with his inborn African accent and then handed over the charge sheet to the Judge.

"Do you all understand the charges as read to you?" The judge asked.

"Yes, your honor."

"Okay. Now, I want all of you to know that you have the right to legal representation. As far as this court is concerned you are all presumed innocent until the State proves you guilty beyond all reasonable doubts. You will have the right to a fair trial by this court and you will have the right to enter a plea, but the court will not take your plea now. Are you clear on all that?"

"Yes, your honor."

"Anyway, you already have legal representation so, I don't need to detail all your rights to you. Your lawyer I guess has already explained all that to you." Charles McCarthy, the British Judge, took time to explain to the accused persons their rights. Voices began to echo in the courtroom and slowly increasing and becoming noisy.

"Order in the court," the interpreter ordered. His voice sounded authoritative, and the noise suddenly ceased. The two men seated on top of the concrete wall took a sharp look at the judge's face, and what they saw was a fairy image of *"Titania and Bottom circa 1790."* The fears showing in his face were so scary, and that prompted them to abandon their seat and decided to walk away. Perhaps, it was for the fear of the possibility of being charge for contempt of court for making noise. They just hate to see themselves in the dock before a huge crowd like this.

The judge noticed it and somehow gave a smile just to assure them not to be afraid of anything which is purely their own imagination. But, they didn't see the smile and so, they simply disappeared from the scene. Minutes later, after the noised had died off, all the witnesses in the case were asked to leave the courtroom.

"All witnesses should please come forward." The clerk announced. 1, 2, 3, 4 . . . Both prosecution and defense witnesses came as announced. "You're requested to leave the courtroom and move to the trees outside. Each one of you will be called upon to come and testify when needed. But until then do not come near the court room when proceeding begins."

The clerk directed, and they all went to the trees in front of the offices of the Land Valuation Board. Close to the courtroom also was the office of the District Assembly as well as the two office rooms building of the National House of Chiefs. The two rooms were inadequate to accommodate a six member staff plus the newly posted Registrar. Inside the office of the Registrar were an old table and a new chair, a large volume of stacked files and other relevant documents packed in a cabinet. There were other files lying on the floor making the office appeared very small in size. Inside the brown cabinet was a file with the title, *"The 1958 Chieftaincy Dispute between the Kunus & the Mawus"* with cobwebs all over it.

The defense witnesses were directed to go to the offices of the NHC while prosecution witnesses were at the other side of the LVB building under the mango tree. The two men who first reported the matter to Yamyolya were also in court to witness proceedings. The prosecution then called its first witness to come and testify. A young lady walked into the witness dock. While in there, she managed to avoid eye contacts with the lawyer and the 2nd accused. She gave her full name to the court.

"My name is Atimbila Awinpok," she said.

"Madam, by what do you swear, is it the Bible, the Cross or the Quran?" The interpreter asked.

"The Cross," she answered. "Okay, kindly raise-up your right hand while holding the Cross and say the following words after me." She did as directed and with her right hand up high holding the Cross she repeated the following words after the interpreter, "I, Atimbila Awinpok do hereby swear before this honorable court, that, the evidence I shall give in this case shall be the truth nothing but the whole truth, so help me God."

The prosecutor, Mr. Mangotiba Tampuri, was on his feet to aid the witness give her evidence. M.T, as he is affectionately known, has been a State attorney for several years and he has gained a lot of experience as a result. He has handled high profile cases for the most part of his career, and he is noted as one of the few State attorneys who hardly prosecute poorly. Uncharacteristic of him, Tampuri chose not to be in his civilian suite—the usual coat and tire and looking like a colonial politician in it. He rather dressed smartly in his black police uniform with his name boldly written on a tag and hooked onto his left chest and a beautiful white woven nylon rope fixed around his right shoulder with four silver stars arranged vertically on both shoulders indicating his rank in the service, a Chief Inspector.

"Lady, could you please give your full name to the court?" The chief inspector asked.

"My name is Timbila Awinpok," she answered.

"What work do you do for a living?"

"I'm a trader, my lord."

"Could you please tell the court exactly what kind of work or trade you do?" He asked and winked his eyes. The witness stood in the dock mute for a while. She seemed wanting as he could not comprehend the blinking from the prosecutor. For a while, she turned and glanced at the press who were very eager to pick any news from her evidence.

"I brew *pito* at Daanore and Kariyama market." She answered. The prosecutor continued to ask the woman brief introductory questions as the judge kept listening to both of them but very attentively to the witness.

"Do you know the accused persons in the dock?" She looked into the face of the prosecutor like her pastor and answered, "Yes I do." As if she was in a Church affirming her vow to her groom, the man she has always loved. "Do you know why you are here?" He asked.

"Yes I do." Her answer drew laughter among the spectators, and it was a combination of different voices that echoed in the courtroom, sounding like a welled coordinated melody. It was sweet, and the Judge seemed to like it but managed to conceal any visible expression in him; he avoided the "yes I do laughter." Awinpok, who was initially surprised at why her answer attracted such a funny laughter, had to join them in laughing because she also found something funny in how they spectators were laughing. Apparently, the witness seemed to have also been incited by the laughter of the old woman who did not really get the gist why her colleagues were laughing but also chose to laugh. Not only did her voice sounded rough and feeble but also, her teeth were not up to thirty-two. All the front teeth were uprooted by 'old age' and the remaining ones were also tainted with cola-nuts. The judge glared at the witness, and she understood what that meant so she immediately ceased laughing.

"Order in the court!" the interpreter managed to bring the situation under normalcy after he had spared them some few minutes to laugh and feel relaxed. Like his boss, he did not partake in the laughter; perhaps, to him there was nothing funny about the answer that necessitated such laughter.

"Ms. Awinpok," the prosecutor resumed, "please cast your mind back to February 17, this year, and tell the court what you know about this case." The silence in the courtroom was now absolute when the witness began to give her evidence; everybody wanted to hear clearly every bit of what she had to say. At least it will enable them to form their own opinions; an opinion that is not based on hearsay. The journalists were more than ready and interested. They were ready for any valuable evidence which she might give to the court so that they could trade with it as news to the public. The lady began to narrate what she knew about the case.

"My lord, a day before February 17 I was on my way to the market when I saw the first accused and two others standing and . . . From the distance I was standing I was inconspicuous so they did not see me and I overheard them talking about the deceased. I heard them discussing their modus operando and so I began to feel suspicious, concern and curious. I therefore decided to stay put and observe. Then, minutes later after the accused had left the scene your honor, I saw Laa-misi who appeared from the other end of the road, the opposite direction to where I was. I saw her join the two men who were with the accused. As a matter of fact I never saw the faces of those two men because they were wearing face masks but I believe they aren't from our village because they do not look like our men." She told the judge. This again generated some laughter among the spectators.

"My lord, that is all for the witness."—Prosecution. Bachela got up from the wooden bench on which he and Sando were sitting, together with the prosecution. The long mahogany bench was designed to carry only four persons, but had to take two lawyers and three prosecution officers because of the lack of more seats. Bachela walked to his clients but said nothing to any of them and then turned towards the witness standing in the dock.

"Ms. Timbila Awinpok do you know that lying under oath is a serious crime and if convicted you could go to jail for not less than two years?" He asked.

"Objection my lord," the prosecutor said.

"My lord I think it's important for me to let the witness understand this important aspect of the law as a witness before I proceed to dwell on her evidence in-chief. It'll be in her interest."—Bachela.

"Objection overruled."—Judge.

"Yes, I do," the witness answered.

66

"Good. Now, in your evidence to the court you said you saw the first accused person discussing with other two people about the deceased. Is that correct?"

"Yes."

"Can you then tell the court who those two are?"

"No. I didn't see the faces of those men and so I can't identify them."

"Madam, I put it to you that none of the accused persons was seen by you at any point in time on that day discussing with anybody about the deceased."

"That is not correct. I saw Zirili and Laa-misi that day."

"Could you tell this honorable court what you claimed to have heard the first accused discussed with the others as you said?"

"My lord, I didn't actually hear all what they were saying but I head them mentioning the deceased name repeatedly in the conversation."

"That is all for the witness, my lord."

On the bases of the evidence as given by the witness, counsel didn't find anything serious implicating any of his clients, not even the first accused as she wants the court to believe. He therefore, did not find it necessary asking more than a few relevant questions that could expose her as an untruthful witness and discredit her evidence. The prosecution second witness was next to come and testify. He also told the court what he knew about the death of Kufugu, and like PW1, there were many inconsistencies in his evidence too. Defense attorney was on his feet again ready to cross-examine the witness. He took off his scholarly spectacle from his face and looked at the man standing. Carefully, he positioned his wig firmly on his head and again looked at PW2 sharply for the second time. He turned to his clients and nodded his head.

He looked at the witness again for the third time as if he was aiming to shoot him down for coming to spread hearsay and lies. It is a hidden technique which he uses sometimes to try to intimidate a witness not to lie but say it to suit his cause. In this case, counsel just wanted the truth, and as usual, he made sure he turned the witness inside-out to get him to contradict himself. After exploring that technique, he made sure he had exhausted all the relevant questions that will expose PW2 as well and brand him as dishonest and misleading. He oftentimes will walk to him at the dock and look directly in his face before asking him a question. The third and fourth witnesses were also called, and in their evidences, they told the court it was PW1 who informed them about what she claimed to have seen and so they also duly hinted the head of the royal clan, Yamyolya.

At about 3:30pm prosecution was ready to call its fifth and final witness to close the case. It was a long day for the Bench, so the judge adjourned the case briefly for thirty minutes. Like him, it was a tiring day for everybody who came, but that notwithstanding, the crowd was still thick and ever ready to wait for the judge to come and resume sittings again. At four o'clock, Justice McCarthy had not yet come to the courtroom. While waiting for him, Bachela decided to engage his clients in a nave relaxing conversation and all the three accused persons were wearing smiles on their faces. Awinpok had also joined prosecution on the long bench, and they also seemed okay as a team. On the other side of the courtroom where the royal elders were seated, a journalist attempted to interview Bunchara. When his attention was drawn to that, M.T cautioned against it and told the journalist to hold on with any interview from any of the royal family for now. He explained that anyone of them could be called as a witness depending on how the case might go and so, he will not want him or any of them to be interviewed on the matter when it is still in court.

At quarter past four, the clerk ushered the judge in and proceedings resumed again. To his surprise, the first accused saw Mr. Nyelba, in the witness dock to give evidence. He seemed to have least expected him to be in the dock claiming to be an eye witness; he just could not understand what he had witnessed as far as the death of his friend was concerned and which he now wants to tell the whole world. Nonetheless, Zirili was not perturbed about it since he trusted his lawyer to be competent enough to do a good job for him.

"Mr. Batesma Nyelba," Bachela called his full name as he was about to take him through cross-examination. He asked the witness to look at the man in the other dock and tell the court whether indeed he knew him.

"My lord, yes I know him," he answered in the affirmative as he successfully avoided looking directly at the face of the accused.

"What about the other two accused persons?"

"I know all of them," he answered.

"Good! Now, could you then tell the court the kind of relationship that existed between you and the first accused?"

"My lord I knew him to be the elder brother of my best friend." At this point, the prosecutor got up and asked the witness to tell the court whom he was referring to as his best friend.

"My lord, I mean the deceased in this case, Kufugu the younger prince." He said, and continued, "Indeed, he was a true friend of mine and . . ."

"Thank you Mr. Nyelba," counsel acknowledged the clarification he made and continued with the cross-examination. "So, how long or how well do you know the first accused?"

"My lord, I knew him the very first time I became a friend to his brother. I think that was fifteen years ago. Yes, fifteen years ago."

"So, can this honorable court take that to mean that you knew both of them very well?"

"Yes my lord that is correct."

"Thank you. Alright, Mr. Nyelba, can you then tell the court what kind of relationship existed between the first accused and the deceased?"

"My lord, I think they had a good relationship as brothers to the best of my knowledge though . . ."

"Did you know for sure that until his death, there was indeed a good brotherly relationship between the accused and the deceased?"

"Objection my lord, my lord the witness has answered the question already, and I do not understand why he is being asked to answer it again,"—MT. The prosecution was of the view that defense attorney is trying to push the witness to change his answer from, "I think" to "I know," so that he could capitalize on that point to make a good argument out of it. He understood most of the questioning tricks of lawyers and he knew that most of the time unfortunately though, most witnesses fall victim to such 'questioning tricks' if not well guided.

"Well, my lord what I am really seeking to do, is just to get clarity in his answer. That is all and nothing else,"—Counsel.

"Objection overruled. Witness is to answer the question,"—Judge.

"My lord, I think they had a good relationship," he answered. PW5 was smart enough to understand the game plan of the lawyer, and why M.T objected to the question. He therefore, stuck to his colors; he refused to be stampeded to change the original answer he gave. Counsel continued with the cross-examination, "Has there ever been any misunderstanding between the deceased and any of the accused persons?"

"My lord I cannot tell."

"Nyelba, you told this honorable court that you were in the accused house with the deceased on February 17, this year, am I right?"

"Yes, that is correct, my lord."

"Good. While there did you eat any food from the house?"

"Yes. The accused, myself and his younger brother the deceased, ate some food prepared by the third accused." "My lord I am done with the witness for today. Thank you," he ended.

CHAPTER NINE

THE SKY APPEARED blue and beautiful at about a quarter to three with the clouds moving slowly like a big ship in the deep sea. The sun was still descending, and the isolated white mass of condensed watery vapor was also hanging in the atmosphere. Slowly, it began sweeping the sun away. The day was not over yet and so the cross-examination continued inside the courtroom, and everybody was very attentive and closely following proceedings as the questions continued to flow. Just a few of those standing outside the courtroom had left and, there was now enough flow of fresh air into the room. The witness was tensed up in the box like condensed camel milk.

"Now, when you left the housed of the accused did the two of you pass elsewhere before going home?"

"Yes."

"Good! Mr. Nyelba, can you please tell this honorable court where you took the deceased to, on that fateful day."

"Objection your honor."

"Objection overruled." The trial judge requested the witness to answer the question.

"My lord, from the house we went straight to 'Zanamat' near the Community Centre. At the Bar, we drank a bottle each of castle milk stout beer after which we left." he said.

Bahcela got a signal from Sando and he walked to him and took a piece of note paper from him containing only one sentence calligraphic handwriting. "*I'm told the witness was dating the third accused then. Thanks*," It read. Bachela looked at it quickly and then walked straight to the witness and said to him, "Mr. Nyelba, this is my last question. Anyway I do not mean to exhaust you here today." Almost everybody in the courtroom began to laugh.

"Kindly look into the face of the lady standing in the dock," he pointed at Laa-misi and said, "tell this court what relationship existed between you and her. Is she your fiancé or not?" He added.

"I object to the question. My lord, really, what is the connection between this particular question and the crime committed? I think if for nothing at all, counsel is trying to invade the privacy of the witness. Moreover, I do not think that it has anything to do with the case." The question seemed huge on the witness head, forcing the head to fall forward. He also looked inflated like an angry frog about to fight a cobra; he seemed ready to invasively answer the question, but Judge McCarthy sustained the objection.

"That is all for the witness, my lord. I pray the court will grant the accused persons bail," counsel concluded. He was very satisfied with the unsatisfactory answers given by all the witnesses to almost all his questions. He therefore was so much hopeful of winning this case.

"Accused persons are each granted a bail of five hundred cedi with one surety to justify. This case is adjourned to May 02." The judge brought proceedings of the day to an end at exactly 5:10pm.

The white clouds on the blue sky continued to converge successfully. The night had just begun, and the streets of Accra were busy as usual and risky, especially around the 'Kwame Nkrumah Circle'. The street lights had been dead for the past seven days, and the city authority seemed unconcern and this gave more room for the street pick pockets to operate smoothly and safely unnoticed. Those who knew the city map very well, would not dare pass around the popular tiptoe lane considering how dangerous that place is always even in the presence of bright street lights.

Few minutes after the court had closed, drops of water started to fall from the sky and everyone began rushing to catch any available *tro-tro* (passenger car) to their various homes. Those who could afford to pay for a taxi went for that, instead. Suddenly, sounds of accompanying thunder storms sent most pedestrians running for safety. A very bright white lightning flew in the sky, followed with a vibrated sound that struck the earth and everything shook. All that notwithstanding, Awule and Lion decided to walk. They carefully followed the route that they considered a minimum risk; they understood very well how dangerous 'circle' could be at that time of the evening, more so at night when the street lights are not functioning—they knew exactly where they were to pass to get to their destination and avoid being a victim of theft. They decided to go to 'Soldier Bar' to wine and dine.

The distance to their destination was quite far and a taxi would have been a more prudent choice but they decided to walk in the drizzling waters. Somehow they just wanted the exercise of walking—not really for the purpose of losing weight but just to improve their health and fitness. Their conversation was gradually ceasing as it began to rain. None of them was interested in talking much. They just walked till they were tired and Awule started zigzagging on the road like a drunk, endangering his life. Fortunately for him, there weren't vehicles plying that road. They just walked, talked and laughed; they walked and talked about their conversation in the courtroom and how the interpreter gave the order, like an ex-service man. They laughed at it. And they even laughed at their own fear when the judge traded a stony looks into their faces which made them to leave the courtroom and joined those outside. They talked about everything and laugh at anything funny they could remember as they continue walking.

They managed to cut corners to avoid passing under the circle overhead bridge, but as they walked closer to their destination they saw three unidentifiable persons standing in front of the Agric. Development Bank in an obscured corner. They instantly became very concerned that the safety in that part of the city also couldn't be taken for granted, so they tried walking faster; they plucked up courage and walked faster than their normal speed. Lion was most of the time a few steps behind Awule, and at times he would even make an attempt to run just to be at par with his friend who had a lot of youthfulness in him. It was not a race anyway, but he did not want to be left behind. The three men took Awule's breath away when they stopped Lion. Fortunately for them the three men only advised them to be extra careful next time when walking in the city because of night criminals. They decided not to take anything from them. The two men were now more confused and tired and needed some rest to enable them to concentrate on their safety and plan on how to dodge meeting people like that since they could also be criminals as well. But probably not like the hungry ones who will not spare even a cedi.

"We are lucky they didn't take anything from us," Lion said as they walked away. Finally, they managed and got to their destination safely in the rain. To his surprise, Lion did not see even a single commercial sex worker at 'Soldier Bar' as it used to be some years ago when the bar was new. The city Authorities chased them off and 'Soldier Bar' was now a lorry station. After standing there for a while, Lion pulled his friend, and they walked across the street into a nearby noise proof building; a nightclub owned by a Lebanese and inside the club was many people. Some were seated while many others danced to the music. It was loud and good. The two decided to join the other four ladies in a salsa dance. They liked the music and the dance, and they liked the ladies too.

It was just ten minutes into the dance when the DJ caused another disc to revolve for the latest *R&B* song and it echoed the following lyrics, *step to the right, step to the left and spin around . . . Step, step, step, step . . .* The crowd danced and sang along while the DJ was busy remixing the rhythms. They all sang and danced till the song died off. Mr. Lion, as he was affectionately called, unintentionally interrupted the conversation between Awule and one of the ladies. After he had finished talking to him, he went and sat at a hidden corner where he could have a very good view at all the ladies in the club. It was a very good **c**oncealed place where he could take any lady by surprise.

"Hi, my name is Lydia," the bar attendant greeted. "Sir we have run out of Don Gassier wine tonight, but I can get you some beer if you wouldn't mind. We also have pasties that could help take care of the rainy cold weather."

"Good! I'm fine with that, dear. Just a bottle of Guinness and I will be alright." He sat there looking weary. He took out some cedi notes from his pocket and placed them on the table. The girl brought the drink and took the money. From nowhere, the lady he met some time ago at the National Theatre came and sat by him unexpectedly; she was about thirty now, but she was still looking younger than her age. She was in her usual pink shirt and a black skirt. The skirt was designed as if with the intention to tempt men, just as how Eve tempted Adam with an apple. The length of the skirt did not go beyond her knee and yet it was cut high to the pelvis which allows it to fall open freely showing her thigh, looking attractive and pleasant to the eyes. Perhaps, she wore that skirt because she knew what men usually would like to see and so she was determined to tempt anyone interested. Lion remembered she had told him five years ago that she came from the north to the city with the aim of becoming a professional dancer but a knee injury had ended her chosen career so early that she was now hopeless of achieving her dream. He could not however, remember her name. The lady noticed that and just laughed.

"Oh no, have you forgotten my name so soon? My name is Love," she said. She had changed her real name since she came to the city, to a western one even though she couldn't feel any pride in her new name.

"Yeah, Love the dancer?" He enquired and gave a sharp smile.

"Yes. Love the professional dancer who never was." She answered and they both laughed tenderly and she blinked her left eye romantically.

"Looking for a good time tonight? Well, I think I should be able to handle you to your satisfaction," she said. Without waiting for a response, Love began to warm up Lion; she voluntarily ran her fingers on his graying temple in the hidden corner and the man felt a rush of excitement inside his veins. She again noticed the excitement in him and therefore, decided to stop; so that she could have the bargaining power in case he was ready to engage her services for that night.

"You have everything that a man needs. At least, from what I can see," he remarked.

"I would take fifty cedis only for a night and hundred for overnight duty but, I don't accept checks. It's cash and carry."

"Oh yeah, that shouldn't be a problem for a man like me."

"That's a good deal, lady. What did you just say your name was?"

"Just call me L.L if you wouldn't mind," she said.

"Well, that's ok but what is the meaning of L.L if you wouldn't mind?" She looked at him straight into the eyes, smiled and said, "L.L is Lady Love and I promise to make it a memorable night for you."

Ok L.L!" "Remember my name is Lion, and there is a reason why my friends call me by that name."

"Well, if you're the Lion I'm the Lioness tonight and I will subdue you."

"Alright, I will hold you to your promise. Do you know the meaning of G-U-I-N-N-E-S-S?" He asked.

"Girls Under Influence Need Nothing Except Serious Sex," she answered, and they both laughed and walked out from the nightclub leaving Awule busy dancing with his four ladies.

From the court, Sando drove the three accused person's home. The old woman also went with them. She came all the way from the village specifically to give her undoubted support to the prince and let him know that at least, not everyone believes that he killed his younger brother. They all went home feeling glee though the three accused persons knew the case wasn't over yet. By the tradition of his people, Zirili is not supposed to go back to Pusig since he was not yet exonerated by either the gods of the land or by the law courts on the crime of murder.

The children were happy to see their parents back home. Little Ngudi went to sit with his mother who was in the living room. He jumped and sat on her mother's lap looking straight into her face and feeling comfortable. Then he rubbed his soft palm on his mother's forehead. "I miss you Mom," he said. The woman felt the love and affection of her child; very tender, genuine and lasting. She in turn also rubbed her palm gently on the little boy's head for a while. "Love you too, son," she told him. After a brief time with the children, she went into the bathroom for a midday shower. At least, to keep her body clean, reduce the stress and feel fresh and renewed.

Minutes later, she came out after the shower and joined her husband who had already finished bathing and was listening to the radio in the sitting room without the children. She sat close to him holding a cup of tea and reading the newspaper she bought on their way from the court. Then she sparked a conversation with her husband who was holding the newspaper. She started talking about everything that had happened in the court and at the police station as well when she was invited for questioning. They talked about the crowd and the royal elders who handed him over to the police. They talked until he began to doze off on the sofa chair, making the conversation one sided and boring. So she started to flip over pages of the magazine she loves to read. One after the other she flipped over till she saw an article which interested her most. The article was about how a woman could maintain her beauty to keep her attractive. She read it several times, over and over till she also began to doze off. The telephone rang, but none of them was interested in answering the call. Perhaps they did not want to talk to whoever it could be.

The woman looked at her watch, and it was 7:02pm. The children had all gone to bed, and she simply did not want to get up from where she was sitting. The telephone rang again for the second time. Then, it rang for the third time. The man got up from the chair to answer the phone call. He dragged his feet reluctantly to the telephone. On the other side of the phone was Sando's voice. The young associate lawyer called to remind them about the date for the next court appearance.

"Could you please turn the volume of the radio a little bit lower after you have finished answering the phone call?" She asked. She always preferred a quiet and undisturbed environment like the swamp mango trees area in the village closed to the posy field near the palace. Knowing that she wanted a quiet time, the man simply turned off the radio completely and went back to the chair.

The accused persons were in court that day and the crowd had increased in number more than the previous court sitting when they were granted bail. The courtroom was once again filled to it capacity with different kinds of people from all walks of life. They all seemed to have the same reason for coming—they came to witness court proceedings involving the prince. The judge walked in wearing the same outfit that he wore the last time with the same unfriendly face. Quickly he sat down looking very busy and ready to dispose of the case. He enquired from prosecution if they have more witnesses to call.

"My lord no more witnesses. Just the investigator and we are done. Thank you." Detective Sgt. Wintima was called to take the witness stand to testify, and the process was brief. After he had finished with his testimony for prosecution, the judge adjourned the case again.

"I'm adjoining this case for a few minutes," he told both the defense and prosecution teams.

"Most grateful my lord," they said.

"All rise!!! Court is adjourned for a few minutes." Upon the command, they all rose up for McCarthy to be ushered into his chamber. For almost forty minutes gone, the judge kept everyone guessing and anxious to know what could be the reason for such an early adjournment. Many therefore, began to wonder and others also began to read meanings into his action. The journalists whispered among themselves, and some were even of the view that the Governor might have telegraph him on the matter. Almost everybody speculated but within the expected time, the judge came back from recess after attending to nature call. He sat down wearing a mean face and tried several times adjusting himself on the chair to a comfortable position as if there was a problem with the chair. The rumbling sound from his stomach was becoming loud as he sat down to adjudicate. The gurgling lasted for less than a minute then the gas began to subside easing the pain he was going through. Again, he adjusted himself one more time backward in the chair and it seemed ok for him. So, he was ready to exercise his authority as the 'master' of the courtroom. He granted the defense counsel the green light to make his closing address on the case after the two defense witnesses had also finished with their testimony.

"Your honor," he said as he began to make a submission of no case on all the charges brought against his clients. "The evidence before you as produced by prosecution witnesses has no credibility worth considering to say the least. I sincerely therefore, do not think that the evidence as adduced by prosecution, really merit the conviction of these innocent accused persons standing before you. My lord, as a matter of fact, I think what the witnesses have been able to do successfully, I must say, is to give conflicting and contradictory accounts and sometimes, confusing themselves as we have all witnessed them come and go one after the other. They most probably came with the aim to throw dust into the eyes of the court, hoping this honorable court will take their words as the truth. Undoubtedly, my lord will agree with me that the prosecution has grossly failed to prove beyond all reasonable doubts to this court that all the three accused persons, jointly or severally charged, or any of them for that matter, could have, might have or indeed have committed any of the offenses for which reason they were brought here before your lordship." He paused as he turned to look at his clients and continued.

"Your honor, this court will be given true meaning to justice if these innocent people are acquitted and discharged since the evidence as presented by prosecution has failed to stand the test of the law in respect to the crime of conspiracy to commit murder and or committing murder as charged."

As he talked, he continued to make eye contact with the judge and knowing very well that a lawyer is like a salesman, he kept his argument brief, direct and aimed at the significant inconsistencies brought out during the trial. At this point, he carefully observed the judge as he was busy writing. He tried to detect any obvious reaction from him—any hint that would allow him to touch on that exposed interest or prejudice if any. Or even capitalize on any of his points that the judge might consider significant so that he will emphasize on those points with great passion. He tried, but, as with most judges, McCarthy remained stone face, well composed and relaxed and busy taking note of relevant points of law. Hence, one hardly sees any such expression of prejudice on his face; he made sure he had concealed his thoughts and emotions very well throughout the trial.

His ability to eloquently argue without using notes, his sweet oratory, and his immersed knowledge on matters of law was worth considering. The crowd loved to hear him make legal arguments. As a seasoned attorney, he knew very well that an argument somehow has more points if the lawyer did not have to refer to notes, it help to give the impression that he intensely believe in everything that he was saying. He knew that and was using it appropriately and advantageously. After destroying the credibility of all the witnesses, he felt reasonably confident of winning the case. The astute lawyer made sure he ended his submission in a more persuasive and convincing manner.

"Your lordship, I therefore pray this honorable court will acquit and discharge the accused persons," he concluded.

On June 02, the dawn cock crowed earlier than the usual time, announcing the beginning of a new day. Few hours after the cock had crowed the sun was seen rising and shining. By noon, the day was bright and hot, and the courtroom was warm. As usual, it was well packed and those who could not get seat to sit down had to hang around outside of the Courtroom. As usual, the old woman was there too. This time she was fortunate to have gotten a place to sit in the courtroom. Obviously, she came earlier just to avoid the phantom of pain she went through in the previous sittings when she could not get a place to sit. This time she had a seat close to the media men where she could see everyone and everything happening in the court. One of the journalists, who have been seeing her in court all the time ever since the case started, decided to interview her. She was in her eighties, and the journalist was thirty-two. The woman obliged and granted the interview. She narrated her ordeal to the young man seated next to her. It started like an informal dialogue between the two but the journalist knew he could make distinct news from it since most of his colleagues will focus on the judgment only. He therefore decided to interview her while waiting for the judge to deliver his judgment.

"My son, in fact, my pain was like an amputated limb. I was confused about everything, starting from the vanishing of our king, the death of the prince and now the prosecution of the man who is the immediate heir to the throne. I'm more than convinced that he will be found innocent. I know his father very well, and I have witnessed the birth of this young man too. I must also say that I don't believe that the Whiteman's law can find the murderer. I can however assure you that, the gods of our land will expose the killer of our son." She said, in an interview.

Justice McCarthy walked into the courtroom fully ready to dispose of the case. He sat down and immediately struck his gavel to punctuate the noise and announce his readiness to give his ruling on the matter. He did not intend to keep the spectators in suspense, so he began reading his judgment as soon as he was satisfied with the level of silence and attention he needed in the courtroom. Delivering the judgment, he clearly enumerated with emphasis some of the inconsistencies in the evidence of the first and third prosecution witnesses as pointed out by defense counsel in his submission to the court. Many times as he continues to read the judgment, he will pause momentarily and take off the reading glasses, look at the accused persons and then continue reading. Sometimes also, he does that when emphasizing on a vital point that exposes any of the accounts of prosecution witnesses that merit dismissal as untruthful.

After reading about two pages of his judgment, he took off his eyeglass and looked at the accused persons in the dock then at the gallery and back at the accused persons, focusing on the third accused. He then wore his eyeglass again and allowed it to hang loose on his face while looking at the accused with his naked eyes. He looked at them just for sixty seconds then positions it well and firm on his face and continued to read the four pages judgment.

"From the evidence as adduced by the prosecution, it is clear that the State has woefully failed to prove beyond all reasonable doubts, that, both first and second accused persons are guilty of the offenses as charged. This court therefore, finds them not guilty of the charges and they are therefore acquitted and discharged on both counts," he ordered. He paused again for a while and continued to read the judgment. Meanwhile, the two acquitted persons walked out from the wooden dock in freedom and happiness boldly written on their faces. The joy on their faces was very visible, and everybody saw it. In spite of that, Zirili and Sugru were concerned and wondering what might happen to the third accused.

Laam stood in the dock looking lonely and nervous. She stood there watching her two colleagues walked away leaving her in a real gloomy silence waiting to hear her verdict too. Every so often she will take a quick, deep breath in then slowly out and then look at her lawyer to see if there is any sign of hope. She continued to look at him, and Bachela also looked at her and then nodded his head but, she could not understand what that meant. Everybody in the courtroom was now getting anxious to hear the final verdict on the third accused. They want to know who was responsible for the death of Kufugu. McCarthy paused momentarily for the fourth time and took a quick look at where the old woman sat with the young journalist. He could see the joy on her face after he had discharged Zirili. It was a feeling of true satisfaction of justice and fair trial being the winner of the day. A true reflection of the Whiteman's law as far as this case was concern. He guessed.

The free couple saw the old woman seated with smiles on her face as they walk towards her, but they did not sit there. They bypassed her and walked straight to Sando who was standing outside the courtroom with other clients. The old woman abandoned her seat and followed them there.

The Judge, dressed in his usual attire of a black suit with black gown over it, he resumed reading his judgment and wearing a stony face after the brief pause. He cleared his throat and finally read the following few words to the accused.

"Ms. Laa-misi, this court has found you not guilty on all the counts as charged. You are hereby acquitted and discharge accordingly." He concluded and struck his gavel on the table signaling the end of proceedings and all of them went home acquitted and discharged.

CHAPTER TEN

THREE MONTHS AFTER his acquittal, Zirili attended the final funeral rites of his late father, the king, but to the utmost shocked of all gathered, he refused to be crowned the next king to succeed his father. Perhaps, his decision emanates from a presage of a clashed in the kingdom between two opposing forces which he does not want to get entangled with considering what he had gone through or, maybe he just did not want to be a king. Most probably also, he just preferred being a nobler and not necessarily a king. Two months after the funeral the prince and his family migrated to the city. His younger brother Tusugu was first to have left Pusig after the funeral. He went and settled in an uninhabited land beneath mountains and named the place Zotinga.

Climatically, Zotinga is a village that is usually cold and windy beginning in the month of October to mid-February and extremely hot from February to April then the farming season sets in May. During the cold season of the year, the children are always by a fireside in the early hours of every morning just to warm up their bodies. They therefore, always made sure they gather enough dried grass and maybe some pieces of wood the previous day to prepare for the accustomed morning 'fire rituals.' Those who would not want to come outside, may choose to be with their parents in their rooms and bundled themselves up with all kinds of clothing and lying on their mats like engaged couples of Wales. These are the privileged ones among the rest. They have the luxury of choosing to stay indoors or join their peers outside.

The feeble orphans usually will assemble in an old woman's room to get the opportunity to warm up themselves with the heat coming from a burning coal pot and often than not they will listen to folktales that imbibe honesty, respect for the elderly, morality and hard work in children.

Also, unlike the privileged children whose parents provide them with clothes to wear and food to eat, the orphan children use warn out cloth to cover their primate parts. Nicely, each one will wrap the cloth around his or her body and tie it around the neck to hold. The art of wrapping oneself in a cloth as a dress takes days of repeated practice to master. Those who do not have cloth or perhaps cannot even wrap themselves, could be seen walking around naked with their genital parts loosely swinging in-between their thighs from one end to the other flip-flopping as they run, especially when playing soccer with 'socks ball' or when playing the night *naa-see* game. 'Socks ball' is made from discarded plastic bags, and rags bundled together with cushion inside the socks and using thread to artistically weave it into a round shape to make a ball. *Naa-see* on the other hand, is a game usually played in the night preferably when there is no moonlight. It is played by two sets of the teams, and usually, a circle is drawn and at least three or four or more people forming one set of team are selected and stationed inside the circle with each holding a twisted cloth with the responsibility to chase and hit members from the opposing team. They do so with the aim of preventing members of the other team from running into the demarcated circle. Members who are not part of the 'circled team,' are supposed to hide in places that they can't be seen to avoid being beaten with the wrapped cloth so that they could secretly run into the circle unnoticed. A member from that team is considered disqualified from the game if he fails to run into the circled within the expected time limit set for the game.

It has been six years now since Zirili left for the city for a permanent stay with his family together with Bakutoma. Mbangiba his mother has been longing for Bakutoma ever since he left to the city with Zirili. One day she decided to travel to the city to see her only son. Two days to the start of the journey she made sure the chief hunter was able to get her enough *bush-meat* to take with her to the city. She also bought some few items for her son as well as for Ngudi, Gabuna, Sapong, and Zumbugri.

As the wife of a canton chief, Mbangiba is known in Pusig by her titled name, *Naa Pua*. She was given two young girls and two muscular bodyguards to escort her to the city. From Pusig, the driver stopped over at Sabongari at her request, to enable them to have a rest. After a brief rest there, they continued the journey to Sabogo. They bypass Mazema and stopped at Zotinga where she spent some time with the people there. Then, from Zotinga they continued to Gingande and then to Tensungo but they did not stop there. She narrated to them the history of the Kumus people and the reasons why Tusugu allowed them to settle in Zotinga together with the other tribes. Throughout the journey she has been telling them the historical significance of each of the villages to the Muwus kingdom. She at times, spoke, but just briefly about the death of the late king, the murder of Kufugu and the prosecution of Zirili as well as the calamity that befell the entire kingdom after the death of the king. She continued to tell them the history of the kingdom till they finally got to their destination.

Sugru was sitting in the living room with Zirili when she heard the doorbell rang. She peeped through the window and saw a lady standing in front of a muscular gentleman at the door. She moved to another window at the opposite side, pulled open the curtain a little bit wider, and from there, she had a good view at them. From that window, she was able to see another lady standing by a white 404 Peugeot car with the registration number UR 787. The doorbell rang again for the second time and she went and opened the door. Upon seeing her walking towards the door, the man gently tapped the young lady, and she also sent a signal to her colleague who was standing by the car. Then she also quickly conveyed the message to *Naa Pua* and the second guard opened the back door for *Naa Pua* to step out from the car. She came out in her queenly dress holding a long brown horse tail; a symbol of her position as a wife of a chief from a royal clan.

She was very happy to have finally gotten to her destination. Sugru gleefully walked to meet her, and the two embraced each other with great pleasure. *"N'naa, n'naa, n'naa,"* She greeted, as the two of them walked with smiles into the house. The children also came out when they heard the voice of *Naa Pua*. Ngudi was first to come out from the house when he saw his mother standing with her guest. Gabuna followed next; he appeared from the garden where he and Sapong were watering the vegetables. Zumbugri happily ran to Bakutoma to announce the good news to him; he made sure he located him from where ever he was and told him about the arrival of his mother from the village. All the children stopped whatever they were doing and joined the guest and her entourage in a joyous mood. Mrs. Zirili made sure her guest was given a befitting protocol treatment of a chief's wife. Being a wife of a prince, she knows and understands the traditional value of a chief's wife and how her guest must therefore be received. But, for the refusal of her husband to be crowned as the next king after the death of his father, Sugru would have been the next queen of the kingdom.

In the dining room together with Zirili, they ate, watched TV and spoke at length on almost everything interesting but dwelled much on events back home. During their conversation, *Naa Pua* told Zirili about the desire of her husband to see all the children home during school vacation which will coincide, with the annual wrestling and *damba* festival to be held in Zotinga.

"You see, since the children are far from home and as you know, the city could be poisonous to their traditional heritage and so we need to make sure that they don't end up being alien to their culture," she opined, and the three of them laughed.

"Well, you are right and we will make sure they come home very often."

"That will be great." She was extremely excited to hear Zirili approved of her wish to see the children in the village but she didn't make it visible.

"What about you? Aren't the two of you coming?" She enquired and again they all laughed.

"Hopefully we will come also," the man answered.

Bakutoma was also happy seeing his mother. He had not seen his parents ever since he left for the city six years ago. He missed them so much that he could not avoid sharing some tears when he was told that his mother will leave for the village the following day. He knew he was no more a child and he also believes that big boys do not cry but, he now understands why sometime they cry. In his case, it is not because of any pain that he feels inside him, yet, he cried.

"The city is a nice and beautiful place to be, but I think the village is a wonderful and peaceful place to live; no vehicular noise, the people are each other's keepers, there are minimal social vices and above all, we know ourselves and can track anyone who commits a crime. Also, unlike in the city, premarital sex and extramarital affairs are shunned in the villages," *Naa Pua* said as she walked towards her car with Zirili who surely seemed to disagree with her on that view. Certainly, not when the culprits who killed Kufugu were yet to be found; not even the gods have been able to do that.

Bakutoma and his colleagues were happy to hear that his father has invited them to the annual wrestling festival. They really will love to be there and they intend to enjoy again every bit of the village life that they've missed so much, especially, the annual *damba* festival and the wrestling contest which is an all adult affair. Usually, in such events the children are first to come to the venue wearing their traditional festive attire—a top coat made from a sheep skin with raffia skirts to cover their bodies. They will sit in a semicircle position and witness the men do the wrestling, the first activity of the day. They will paint their faces with black and white colors and each one of them will have to carry a stool for an elder person to sit and watch the wrestling. The fight is usually between wrestlers from the Mawus and the Kumus tribes drawn from all the nine villages namely, Sabogo, Sabongari, Gingande, Possum, Natinga, Sabon-Zongo, Mazema, Patelme, and Daduri. The most beautiful women from each of the villages are selected and anyone who wins the wrestling contest will choose his preferred wife from among the nine women. The aim is to encourage intermarriages amongst the two ethnic tribes and also foster unity among them.

Besides marrying through the power of your strength in a wrestling contest, another unique thing about Zotinga which is rare in the city is that there is no such thing like dating amongst the young adult. The normal way to meet a lady for marriage is when she is given by her parents to the other family in mutual consent from the parents of both the man and the woman. However, although there is no formal dating, two young people in love may be allowed to take a walk together sometimes, but the best opportunity for spending time together is at a public gathering especially during festive seasons like *damba* festival, a wrestling contest or at a funeral or when the adults are likely to be in the village square just having a good time with friends. Most of the young men, however, prefer getting their future wives by winning a wrestling contest. It really makes them feel proud. Not only do they get the needed recognition and respect from their peers, but also from the entire community as well.

Another thing which is very rare in the city and which Bakutoma and his colleagues will like to experience again is cattle herding. The village folks are usually overjoyed because there is never a short supply of milk, and it's at this time of the season that they usually get meat to eat when the unlucky cow is killed. Particularly interesting in the village during this time is the annual hunt for ticks—the blood sucking insect pest. The insects normally suck the blood of the host cow until it is shaped like a round reddish ball. The kids will then pluck the engorged insects for a feast. They will roast it into a delicacy. The art of roasting ticks was well ingrained in a boy at least by age eight and above. When roasting a tick, one must be careful not to allow too much or too little heat because the tick would burst when overheated or it will be a mess when the heat is too little. These and many more were what Bakutoma and his colleagues have missed badly ever since they left for the city. It is an experience they would never have in the city, and so they happily look forward to be in Zotinga during the festive season when schools vacate.

It was almost a week since schools had vacated for the third term holiday break and though, *Naa Pua* had made a request for the children, they were not certain if the man would allow them to travel to the village. Therefore, the request made by *Naa Pua* notwithstanding, the children will still need to apply for permission to travel before they would be allowed to travel to the village. This has been the established rule in the house. For Bakutoma, he needed it more than any of his colleagues. He hoped to spend much time with his mother who cherishes him so much so that, sometimes his father gets angry with him for no apparent reason. He was now a grown adult who would not want to get so hooked with his mother again like before.

At noon after church, the four children convened a meeting to formally apply for permission to travel to the village. Bakutoma was chosen as the spokesman and was mandated to make a request on their behalf considering that he was the only one who could speak the English language better than his colleagues. On that Sunday afternoon, Zirili was with Sugru seated in the living room. They both glued themselves on the long sofa chair watching their favorite show on TV African network. After sipping a cup of water to cool and maybe smoothing his dry throat. Bakutoma came out from the kitchen seemingly prepared to meet Mr. & Mrs. Zirili. He signaled Gabuna and Zumbugri as soon as he came out of the kitchen, indicating his readiness to go. In return, they smiled at him, and that alone was enough to inflate his confidence level. Funny though, just after he took his first, second and was about to take the third step towards the living room, he heard Sugru sneeze. He quickly took two steps backward in a visibly tensed mood. Gabuna then decided to stay put at the hallway watching while encouraging him.

"Go, go, go," he said. "Go, Daddy will be happy that at least you can speak better English than any of us, and I am sure he will approve our request. Just go," he added. Bakutoma then tried to marshal his confidence again. All that notwithstanding, just after initiating another move forward, he heard a sound of footsteps coming from the living room and again he pulled a fast break and stood there still like a chameleon that has escaped from being knocked down by a moving vehicle in the middle of a road. He told Gabuna that his decision to pull a break was to enable him reassure himself of his ability to do a good job before talking to Dad.

"Oh no, so with all the encouragement I gave you, you still need to boost your confidence level?" Gabuna queried. He seemed disappointed but he wisely concealed it from him.

"What encouragement are you talking about?" Bakutoma angrily asked.

"Look, I need to do that to rekindle my confidence. Do you think it's just easy to go like that when Sugru is there with him?" He pulled a long face and threatens to stop it if he'll not be allowed to take his time before walking to them.

"Okay, okay, okay. I . . . , I . . . I will not say anything again. Okay!" He laughed and gave him a tap at the shoulder. Bakutoma then calculated his steps again with much confidence and regally walked into the living room. Sugru incidentally stared at him concurrently, making him a little bit nervous and deflating his confidence again. Aside Ngudi who was still being pampered by his parents and therefore, could feel free and relaxed when talking to any of them, his colleagues on the other hand always entertain fear when talking to any of them or both of them. This was so because they were always intimidated by the unfriendly and very discipline looks on their parents faces.

At the far end of the living room, was a big writing desk and placed on it beautifully were portraits of Tohazie, Kpognumbu and Gbewaa. Aside those portraits of his father and grandfather, the portrait of Tohazie his great grandfather, the red hunter, was purely an imaginary art work base on a vivid description given by legends. Nobody could have had his photograph at that time since they were no cameras then.

The spokesman decided to make the request to Sugru instead of Zirili. Perhaps, he knew very well that the woman's word would be the final one even if he makes the request to the man.

"Good afternoon Mama." He greeted and began to speak his so-called 'good' English, unmindful of the harm he might cause to the Queen's language. He was known among his peer in school and admired by many for using 'big' words like tintinnabulation, gargantuan, etc. to the delight of his colleagues.

"Mama, I've come to remind you that all of us," he paused and then hit his palm on his chest with pride and said, "myself, Ngudi and our other colleagues would like to migrate from the city to Zotinga for the annual wrestling contest now that we're on vacation. My colleagues have unanimously elected me with confidence to come and inspirationally advance our wish to journey to the village. We are humbly pleading to you, for your merciful permission to travel to the village for the damba festival. Personally it will be a gargantuan wayome honoured if you give approval

to our request. Thank you." He concluded and was very satisfied with his well-rehearsed 'good' English.

Like the lizard who decided to praise himself by nodding its head up and down and saying "well done, well done, well done" for falling down from a tree unhurt, Bakutoma also patted himself on the back, saying, "I think I've done well." He stood there right in front of the woman in suspense but with a strong hope of getting a favourable response from her.

The woman kept quiet; no word of approval or disapproval. She just glared at him seemingly irritated.

"Please could you go and repeat what you just told me to your father? Maybe he can understand your grammar." With that criticism of his English, he began to feel demoralized as he continued to stand before her. "Z, did you just hear what your son said?" She asked the man and laughed teasingly at Bakutoma. He turned and walked to Zirili who was busy cleaning the portraits of the three legends. He stood in front of him and just as he was about to open his mouth to say a word to him, Z stopped him immediately and said, "I know what brought you here, my son. Tell your colleagues to get prepared so that on this coming Saturday, I will take you to the State Transport station to catch the early bus to the village. Is that okay!"

"Yes, uncle," he answered and happily left the scene. Sapong and his other colleagues had already started jubilating before he could even tell them the good news. They heard their father okaying the request.

The journey started on that Saturday as promised, and it was expected to be a tiring long journey with the STC bus. The dilapidated roads were still the same as it was six years ago, compelling the driver to make mandatory stops over at each of the thirteen rest stops for the passengers to have a little rest, and also for the station engineers to work on the bus before they could continue. Nonetheless, they finally got to their destination on time. This year's annual wrestling contest coincided with the traditional *damba* festival and all the canton chiefs from the various tribal groupings converged at Natinga, the chief's palace with their council of elders and subjects. They all came, well dressed in their smocks befitting the occasion and riding their horses. Before the start of the celebration, the paramount chief together with the chief priest of the land came and performed some rituals to give thanks to *gbanwaa* (the superior god), for granting them a good farming season with peace and fostering unity among them. Two red bulls, three white cockerels, a tail of a lion, an elephant foot and one crocodile egg were the items used to perform the rituals.

Soon after the rituals had been performed, all the wrestlers from all the villages then grouped and were ready to lock horns. The selected beautiful women were also showcased to the wrestlers before they started to wrestle and the aim is to entice and motivate them to go into the contest knowing that, the price at stake is worth wrestling for it. The *damba* dancers also grouped themselves and ready to ignite the crowed with a brilliant show of cultural heritage. In their beautiful smocks with two or one horse tail in their hands and a big towel on their shoulders, they assembled at the playground one after the other upon hearing the sound of the drum of the *lung-naa* (chief drummer).

All was set after they had all assembled and so the show began. The drummers played the drums while the women sang, and the dancers danced. Sometimes the women will join the men and dance alongside. Others however, were just fanning their favorite dancers as they dance or sit while waiting for their turn to dance. They danced and danced till they all run out of energy. It is usually in events like this that those with super natural 'black powers' show the stuff they are made of in the village. The four city guys led by Bakutoma were there to witness the wrestling and the *damba* dance as well. They were in their coffee jean pants, dark brown long-sleeves shirts and black shoes to match. No traditional attire. This was meant to distinct them from their colleagues who never wore jean pants before.

One needed to be in the village so as to be able to understand and feel the occasion. Ending the day activities, five muscular palace guards led by the chief warrior, came with their guns to exhibit the military skills and might of the warriors. They also showed the people how ready and well-armed they were to go to war and defeat an enemy in the event of a war. From a distance, the naked upper bodies of the guards look shiny and silky like a well-oiled *tubani* (baked bean). Everybody who came there went back home happy and proud for being part of the annual festivity. This year's wrestling contest was won by a Kumus, and he chose a beautiful Mawus lady to be his wife. They came, they saw and they left with good memories of Zotinga and the city guys really enjoyed their two weeks stay there. They left back to the city fully satisfied for accomplishing their desire of a renewed taste of village life after six long years.

Bachela was not in the country during the festivity. He was in London for a brief stay. On his return home however, he went to the village to greet his people. On his third day in Zotinga, he went to the HIM Bar with his friends where he narrated to them his experience in the Whiteman's land.

"It was a thirteen hour journey by road from Zotinga to the city and a six hour airborne from the city to London. We left Accra a few minutes to 12am, and at exactly six o'clock ante meridiem the plane had safely landed at the Heathrow International Airport; one of the beautiful airports in Europe as I was told. Like a bird in the sky, the flight was simply superb and smooth in the air. Hey, as you are all aware, that was my first time in a plane—and the experience, anxiety, pride, excitement, etc. was just unbelievable. As a matter of fact, it was also my first time experiencing and having a feel of what and how winter is. This chilly and cold weather called winter is not a friend to almost everybody but, it is particularly disliked by the aged as well as those with rheumatism. Frankly, not even the young ones who are born there like it. I guess you can imagine what I went through. Trust me, it was very terrible for me and in fact, I must say that winter had no mercy for anyone. Not even those who were born in it could withstand it. On my first day, I remember being excited about it even though I was shivering immediately I got out from the airplane. Somehow I was enjoying it but as the days went by it became a big problem for me," they all laughed and he continued.

"This was in the early days of November and it's usually at this time of the year that winter sets in. Hmm, I remembered when I told McZee, my white friend, that in Africa and particularly in Zotinga we call it hamattan he and his colleagues laughed at me and in a typical British ascent he asked, "What is haa-mat-tan?"

"...And how did you explain that to him, lawyer?"

"Hmm, well, I just told him hamattan is 'Africa winter' which comes angrily with the wind and dust of the Sahara desert." His answer sparked a long laughter and it echoed in all the four corners of the bar.

"I really like everything about the Whiteman's land," he added. There was a sharp and complete pause, and silence as well, for about two minutes and they looked at each other faces as if they never knew each other. He continued, "So, as I was saying, from the airport we took an underground train from the city of London and journeyed to Milton Keynes. Again, that was my first time experience being in a train. Hmm, another funny thing happened while I was entering the train but I will not tell you people." Again, laughter erupted and he also laughed.

"Hey lawyer, so you also could get lost at a train station. Hmm . . ." one of them remarked.

"It looks funny the way you people laugh anytime I talk of my first experience. Which of you here have had such an experience before?" he teasingly asked and continued to tell his story.

"So, at MK, McZee took me to the popular Nandos restaurant at X'Cape, not far from 13 Bossiney Place, Fishermead, where he lives. At Nandos we ate chicken tikka and French fries, fried rice and chicken broccoli with pepper sauce. That was also another first experience; and I did enjoy it." Again they laughed, but this time just for a short while. Bachela narrated his entire two weeks experience in Europe to his friends and brought lots of excitement in them.

"Bar man! Please bring more drinks. Also remember to tell *M'mabia* to bring us more kebabs, hot ones for that matter with lots of anions. This is Africa and not the land of our colonial masters. Indeed, it's great to be an independent Nation." He added.

In pronouncing the word, onions he replace the alphabet 'O' in the beginning of the word with 'A' in his effort to give a British accent to it. This again sparked laughter when they noted that, the two weeks British man, has suddenly tried to colonize his own accent with that of the Whiteman ever since he came back from London. He continued to share his experience with his friends.

"As a matter of fact, I saw beautiful buildings like the Premier Inn—a multipurpose big shopping mall, and the Jury's Inn where one could locate the popular Ha-Ha Bar and Grill, the Mid-summer House, the Acorn House and many more beautiful buildings. The roads, the restaurants, shopping malls, landscape and indeed almost anything that I had seen was beautiful and the ladies too, hmm. You know what I mean."

"*Nabia* (prince) we know. You don't need to tell us the rest for, it's in the blood." One of them said and they all laughed.

"Over there in London, because of the winter I usually start my day with a cup of hot tea with some scramble eggs spread over brown bread. The hot tea is to keep my body warm. As the day passes by, the winter keeps getting worse for a new person like me."

"But you *paaa*, lawyer you never told us what crumble eggs are," Awusuu queried.

"Well, my brother it's not crumble but scramble and it's basically what we call here fried eggs." This again sparked laughter. Bachela's experience in the Whiteman's land was so interesting and appetizing to the extent that, almost everybody had expressed the desire to visit Europe one day before they join their ancestors in the next world.

CHAPTER ELEVEN

F OR OVER 200 years, starting with chief Ali Atabia in 1721, the Mawus have been chiefs of Zotinga. They have peacefully coexisted with the Kumus dating as far back as the genesis of Zotinga when God created Adam, as a Mawus and Eve as a Kumus, and brought them together as one people with one common destiny; the common destiny to live together peacefully as one united people. In 1958 however, the peaceful coexistence between these two tribes began to hit the rocks when the Kumus laid a claim to the throne and with the support of the then government, chief Bagura was chosen by the Kumus as the chief of Zotinga. His appointment as a chief happened after a committee was appointed by the colonial Governor to look into their claim. In applying the law after the committee had finished with its work, the Governor ruled that the Kumus should be recognized as owners of Zotinga and therefore, they should be the heir apparent of the throne and not the Mawus.

It all began when the Kumus youth revolted against the Mawus right to the Zotinga throne as an exclusive preserved right of the Mawus. This move by the Kumus and with the support of the government, sparked strife between the two tribes over the right to the Zotinga throne. It is believed that the government of the Courageous People's Party got itself involved in the matter because the Mawus did not support the party during the struggle for an independent State.

The appointment of Bagura as a chief was however met with resistance from the Mawus who refused to recognize him as such, stating that chief Salma is the legitimate chief from a royal clan whom they owe allegiance to. This did not go well with the government since it was considered as usurpation of authority hence, chief Salma was warned to stop presenting himself as a chief or else, he will be arrested and prosecuted. This threat forced him to go to exile at Togo where he died nine years later. In that same year that he died, thus in 1966, the government was toppled in a coupe d'état by the Nation Liberators Council and Bagura was dismissed as a chief and the Mawus were once again given the right to appoint a chief, and Zangbeo was therefore chosen as the new paramount chief of Zotinga with the power to also appoint canton chiefs in the various cantons. He ruled for fourteen years and died in 1981.

In December 31, 1981, a new government came to power through a coup d'état. The People's National Dreams Council government, also restored the Kumus to their original status and chief Bagura was therefore, reappointed to his original status as a chief. The Mawus were however refused the right to perform the funeral rites of the late chief Zangbeo. The refusal was against the customs and traditional practices of the Mawus and this therefore disabled them from also appointing a new chief, and this resulted into a violent conflict between the two opposing tribes in 1983; the first conflict ever, since the chieftaincy strife between the Mawus and Kumus began in 1958. In 1984, after the demise of chief Bagura, his funeral was performed and his elder son, Bagura II, ascended to the throne.

On one early morning in March, two years after his ascendency to the throne, the weather in Zotinga was foggy and as cold as a fish locker. It was a strange weather condition and the people have never experienced it before. The coldness was so intense that it nearly almost interrupted the celebration of the Kumus festival. By noon, on that Thursday the weather began to get warm and normal, making way for a beautiful day for the celebration of the festival. At 1:00pm the people started arriving from neighboring villages into Zotinga. Even though unlike the Mawus who usually ride on horses to their festivals, the Kumus were not familiar with horse riding. Nonetheless, they had a good way of assembling at the festival ground. While the women walked from their homes, far and near to the Community Centre, the men in their beautiful smocks rode on bicycles and motor cycles to the festival ground and those who could carry their wives along with them on the back of their bicycles did so with pride.

Food was in abundance that day in every household because everybody had cooked. They were all happy; the children were happy because they would have more than enough food to eat. At least, for the next one week and even have some left for the *garibus* (the surplus collectors).

The women were happy because it is only on occasions like this that their husbands will willingly and happily give them a reasonable amount of money to cook a descent and delicious meal for the family. To the men folks, for the simple reason that they are able to give their wives everything that was requested for the feast, that was more than enough reason for them to be proud of and so, everyone was indeed happy. Happy because everybody that day somehow had a reason to be happy, including some of the Mawus who were also happy to see the Kumus in their smocks as they try to exhibit their mastery in their newly invented festival dance called *bu-la*. They happily and proudly danced to the traditional *googe* (guitar) rhythms with pride. They sang along with *Akitiwaa* and danced bula. A dance that the dancer mostly uses his legs and waist more than any part of the body and it consumes a lot of energy from the dancer. It is a dance that is not suitable for the feebler. The men dance beautifully together with the women in the torrid weather and they were sweating profusely. The pageantry was unique. They were all happy and everybody danced.

The chieftaincy rivalry between the tribes unfortunately was increasingly becoming more acrimonious each day, and to such an extent that it even sparked a violent conflict the day of the festival. It all started at the Zotinga Community Centre right in front of the Police Station when the tribal conflict between the Mawus and the Kumus irrupted again for the third time. Before the conflict started, a man many people best describes as a 'radical by nature' went on the stage and addressed the thick crowd. He spoke to the people and inspired the youth to continue with the struggle for dominance in all spheres of live as far as Zotinga was concern.

"It's our land and we have to control our land and not to allow 'strangers' to rule us," he said. "The struggle for our emancipation must not end here just because we're now the chiefs of our land," he paused and turned and looked at him with smiles. Chief Bagura II smiled back and the lady behind him was busily fanning.

"Chieftaincy is not our only ultimate goal. It was just a priority. Ascending on the throne as a chief is not only what we need but also, we need education, we need to control businesses, dominate in both local and national politics and take our own destiny into our own hands. My dear brothers and sisters, yes it is true that we used to be their 'servants'. We took care of their horses; we farmed for them, they married our mothers and sisters etc. etc. But I must say this, henceforth, starting from today and now the time has come for us to understand that those things are not what we must do forever for them. We have to fight for our dignity and destiny. We must fight for our land. The struggle for independence by the first president of our country was meant to be the struggle for our independence as well; the end of the rule of the minority over the majority, the end of colonialism over independence, the end of the Mawus control of this land over the Kumus." He told the crowd and everybody was happy to hear him say that.

The youth applauded and shouted to his name, "Ndii, Ndii, Ndii, Ndii." He was the hero of the time and they admired the radicalism and revolutionary spirit in him. They hailed him for the inspiration, hope, freedom and the dignity he brought to them. They just love him. They love him because he has awakened them to the realization of the need to fight against inferiority complex and also claim a dignifying status in the revolving history of Zotinga.

Standing under a tree behind the Community Centre and close to the cola nut market were, two armed young men each holding an AK47 rifle and very alert to pull the trigger. The identity of the men was also not known. It was therefore difficult to tell whether they were part of the Mawus warrior group or some of the Kumus Warriors, ready to . . . These and many more questions were difficult to find answers to. The security personnel deployed there to make sure the celebration was peaceful did not see those two armed men. Perhaps, it was due to the lack of vigilance or, they just did not see anybody as a threat to public peace.

According to the Zotinga police commander the presence of the security men was necessary because they have intercepted a letter allegedly written by the Mawus youth threatening to destabilize the events with the claim that the government had denied them their right to perform the funeral of their late chief. An allegation the Mawus vehemently denied and they made sure they criticized the government for perpetrating and aiding injustice.

"This is our land, the land of our birth." Ndii continued to address the crowd. "It is your land, he said, "The land of our ancestors and no one can take it away from us. We will fight for what is ours and we must be ready if so necessary, to let blood flow on all the corners and streets of this land in our quest for our freedom. Even today, we must be ready to fight if the need be." he concluded.

The two armed men who were hiding, were just waiting for a signal so that they could pull the trigger. Minutes after he had finished with his speech, chief Bagura was driven home, and the dignitaries also left soon after the chief had left. There and then, one of the men pulled his trigger and the first gunshot of the day was fired into the air and it sounded rapid.

"That's a sound of an AK47, sir." The body guard drew his attention to it.

"Okay that's good. Just be alert. I'm aware of it but, tell the driver we're going back to the city, okay!" He instructed.

"Yes sir."

The guitarist was still singing, loud and clear and the dancers were vigorously doing a great dance; turning and twisting their legs and waist. They surely seemed to be unaware of what was happening so they were just busy dancing and enjoying the festive mood after the dignitaries had left. Ten minutes after the first gunshot, a second one was fired and this time it sounded like a G3 rifle. No one could tell who pulled that trigger either. Not even those who fired the first warning shot with the AK47 could tell. Both tribes began to be suspicious of each other. Another gunshot sounded again after the G3 and this time it was an M16 rifle. These immediately sent fears to the crowd and the women began yelling and wailing. They began to ran, and they all ran for their lives. The gunshots brought everything that was colorful about the festival to an abrupt end, and it was still not clear whether those two men with Ak47s are Kumus or Mawus, neither was the identity of those who fired the G3 also known. Suspicion, fear, anxiety, looting and burning was the situation.

Many people noticed an unusual day and were curious to understand why gunshots were been fired. They could not comprehend how things could just turn sour in the peak of such an eventful day with heavily deployed security personnel. Minutes later, news instantly flew round to the elders of both tribes about an imminent conflict. The Kumus blamed the Mawus for destabilizing the celebration of their festival. The Mawus on the other hand also blamed the

Kumus for using their festival to incite and start a violent conflict. The blame game was never to end even though the situation was brought under control by the military.

The Mawus decided to consult the oracles and so, quickly Bunchera was instructed to go and inform the priest about the attack by the Kumus. He jumped on his bicycle, and off, he went and in less than an hour he was seen visibly sweating and panting on his way back like a well digger of the tropics. He came and delivered the message from the priest. He had asked him to inform the elders that it was too late for him to stop the bloodshed. The elders were alarmed by the message and so, in less than few hours' news got to the Mawus youth to get prepared for a war against the Kumus the next day. The day came and as they were preparing to go for the war, a woman came outside from a house at Mazema in the heat of all the uncertainty. She saw from afar burning dark flames pushing its way through the windows of a house and also on top of the roof in large volumes into the sky. She quickly ran into another house where some of the Mawus youth had gathered. There, she saw one of them panting like a scared rat who managed to escape from a pursuing cat. She told them about the burning house and the voices of war songs that she heard from afar.

At the St. Anthony primary school also, thick smokes and flames were seen gushing from some of the houses ascending into space. Sounds of rapid gunshots continued to be heard late in the afternoon of that day. It sounded like songs with pop beats; very sweet but terrific. The women and the children were wailing and crying except, the youth and some of the energetic old folks from both tribes who could be seen holding weapons and running to the battle field to fight. They continued to fire gunshots sporadically into the air and everybody was running. The market women, the cattle dealers, drivers, and also school pupils were all running helter-skelter, zigzagging and crisscrossing each other. They were just running, running away from bullets they can't see; stray bullets flying all over in the air. They just ran to any place they could find safety. Teachers also ran for their lives. Shop owners were busy closing their shops. The gunshots continued to be fired disorderly and the whole village soon became engulfed with smoke and gunshot noise.

"Chooo-bui! Yei!! Choo-bui!! Yei!!!" The warrior repeated for the third time "Choo-bui!!" And the crowd responded to it "Yei." Their voices echoed very thunderous.

"Let's go!!! He said. The charged youth were motivated by their war leader to be brave and meet the Kumus at the battle ground. It is always difficult to tell which of them started the war since both tribes will accused each other for sparking it and deny knowing anything about it. They fought, killed each other, burned houses, shops, and virtually destroyed almost anything belonging to any of them. This was the third major conflict between the two tribes.

Aside these three major conflicts which occurred in 1983, 1984 and 1985, they fought again for the fourth, fifth and sixth time. Also, there have been several small but extreme deadly skirmishes over the years after the last major conflict. The hatred between these two tribes was so poisonous that, at times just a simple disagreement between a Mawus cattle dealer and his Kumus counterpart was enough to trigger a fight between the two tribes. Most often than not, politics is what always divide and create tension among the people more than anything else resulting in political violence which then eventually leads to ethnic conflicts. This was always so when it comes to partisan election to elect a representative to serve them in the national legislature. However, this time around it wasn't politics but, nonetheless for over twenty years now, the armed conflict was now like a ritual in the land and for that reason, Zotinga has not known peace neither has it seen any new developments.

CHAPTER TWELVE

O N ONE WEDNESDAY morning at about 8:25am, eight years after the return to constitutional rule, news about the arrival of the presidential candidate for the Nasara People's Party began to trickle in but it was not until 2:00pm when he finally came. The jubilant crowd was shouting his name happily like a savior has been born. They were excited not only because he was coming to tell them his campaign promise, but simply because they were just happy that party politics had come to stay with them. For the Mawus in particular, this means a lot as far as the chieftaincy dispute was concerned. They believe it is an issue still worth looking into and their party, the Nasara People's Party if voted to power will surely help them regain the throne back to where it belong.

His entrance into Zotinga that day for a political rally was superlative. J.A as he was popularly known by his party faithfuls, had a closed door meeting with the Zotinga party elders before he headed straight to the rally ground, where he mounted the stage to address his teaming fans. He was very deep black in complexion with oversize eyeballs, tall and huge, but gentle looking with a thick voice. He was a very cool and a real gentleman. On the stage, the MC handed over the microphone to him after he had introduced him to the crowd.

"J.A, J.A, J.A, J.A, the people echoed his name joyfully and sang the new song that was specially compose for him as a victory song.

"J.A Kuntoye, Kuntoye, J.A Kuntoye, Kuntoye, J.A Kuntoye . . ." Everyone at the rally sang along to the tune with great voices when the DJ played the song. They really like it. Holding the microphone on his left hand he raised his right hand and waved at the crowd, responding to the thunderous cheers from the masses who gathered to listen to him. As far as the Mawus were concerned, it will mean nothing if his presidency will not re-visit the chieftaincy dispute between the two tribes to determine which tribe is, or should be the rightful heir to the Zotinga throne. These are some of the assurances they were eager to hear. As a season politician, J.A knew exactly what his supporters would want to hear him say and he knew what he must do to get their votes. He also understood that he will need not only the Mawus if he is to win the election.

"J.A, J.A, J.A, J.A," they continued to shout his name. He nodded his head up and down slowly like a lizard acknowledging praises.

"Thank you. Thank you. Thank you," he said with his usual deep voice and it succeeded in fading out the noise from the crowd, to enable him deliver his campaign message which might have less or no sincerity in it as it is always common with most politicians.

"Gaa ice water. Ruwan sanyi a-sey a-sha. Ice water," (This is ice water. Ice water, buy and drink. Ice water) the little girl shouted into the crowd looking for people to buy her water. She was still in her school uniform while selling the ice water. Perhaps, she had no time to change into her regular house attire after she came from school. She probably also didn't eat either before her mother put the plastic bucket full of water on her head to go to the rally ground and sell. Since every business person couldn't afford to miss this opportunity to make money on such an occasion, she had to go and sell water to help her mother pay her school fees and take care of other bills as well. She was three years old when her father was killed in one of the conflicts, and since then she and her mother have been selling water to make earns meet in order to survive since no one was taking responsibility to help them ever since she lost her father in a war.

After he had succeeded in bringing down the cheers from the crowd, he then began to speak. *"Kuli-kuli-du, kuli-kuli-du,"* he shouted the party slogan and the crowd also responded back, *"azaa-niye.* "My brothers and sisters, I bring to you greetings from all the regions. The people of the Volta region greet you all. Today my message to all of you is very simple. This year, this year, this year," he repeated and continued, "Ghanaians have decided they will vote the . . . Everywhere I went with my campaign team the people are saying they want the . . . to come to power so that they will get true freedom and jobs. I can assure all of you that there will be no more selling of ice water on the streets by our children who need to be in school learning." The little girl instantly became happy when she heard the message. "There will be no selling of dog chains by our youth, the future leaders of this country and our graduates will not need to sit at home hopeless about their future. We will create jobs by boosting the economy and bringing inflation down to a single digit. It is going to be the golden age of business." He paused and shouted, *"Kuli-kuli-du, kuli-kuli-du,"* and continued, "When we come to power, my government will make sure we create jobs for the youth of this country. Under my government, graduate unemployment will cease to exist completely." He assured them again.

"Yeirrrr . . ." The crowd shouted, and J.A paused to allow the cheers to echo. "To you the people of Zotinga I can say I know and I understand very well the problem at hand here. I know the chieftaincy dispute in this village is as old as the independence of this country. I can assure you people that if you vote our party to power, I will make sure the truth about the Zotinga chieftaincy is established and brought to light once and for all. You see, one thing I know about truth is that, it is like a pen cap and no matter how deep you submerge it into the sea, it will always stay afloat. It just cannot be hidden, and I think that is the situation here in Zotinga. There is no truth," he said. The cheers became more alive and very loud. It vibrated rhythmically for a long time preventing him from continuing with his speech so he allowed them to end the cheers before he continued.

"In my first hundred days in office, I will instruct the National House of Chiefs (NHC) to revisit the matter. Government has no business handling chieftaincy disputes. The Law courts are there." He told the crowd exactly what they wanted to hear, and the cheers were very electrifying and thunderous. The jubilant crowd, mainly dominated by the Mawus, could not hide their joy upon hearing the message of hope from a potential president of the Republic. They were ostensibly trigger-happy by the message from J.A Kuntoye, and so they never even bothered to take a minute and asked themselves if there is any sincerity in his promise, or if indeed that was possible under his presidency, or even if he can really do it. Perhaps, somehow it might be that of obsession on their part. Indeed, they were truly happy when he assured them of letting the

National House of Chiefs and the courts handle the matter. They believed that, justice has eluded them for over twenty years and therefore, it is very reasonable to vote for him and they believed him too. They believe he can do it, and they believe he will not disappoint them. He ended his political speech with shouts of the party slogan one more time. *"Kuli-kuli-du, kuli-kuli-du,"* and the crowd responded, *"azaa-niye."*

They were just fully satisfied with the message from J.A. and they have always had the strong belief that if the chieftaincy dispute were tolerated in the Law courts anytime and in any day, there was no way the decision will not be in their favor. They kept echoing the fact that they proudly traced their roots to Tahazie, the red hunter, and that they migrated from Malle as hunters to Zamfara in Northern Nigeria and later to Pusig led by Gbewaa, the late king. According to them, after the death of the king, his children moved out of Pusig and Tusugu came and founded Zotinga. They also made the claim that the first village to have been founded by their forefathers was Natinga, then later Tensungo, Sabonagri, Patelme, Gingande etc. all in their effort to expand Zotinga and that they established chiefdom there hence; they were the first people to have occupied the throne with chief Ali Atabia as the first chief of Zotinga. The Mawus have also always advanced an endless argument that there are historical facts to support the claim that they were first to have settled in Zotinga, and also established a customary process for choosing a chief. According to them this was to ensure that the right person is chosen from among them and to avoid any dispute, as currently is the case between them and the Kumus.

In one of his appearances in court on behalf of the Mawus, thus, after J.A had won the election and have fulfilled his promise to let the courts handle the matter, Bachela explained to the court in his submission that the wisdom behind the establishment of the mode of choosing a chief to the throne was because chieftaincy as they knew it to be has no end and for that reason there must be a way of perpetuating the legacy to avoid any possible abuse of the institution such as what had happened in 1958 or is happening now whereby politicians meddle into chieftaincy matters.

"Even the Queen of England is aware of our claim and can attest to the fact that the Mawus are the only people with the exclusive right to the Zotinga throne because they started it all," he said.

He also explained that the established traditional practice of the Mawus for one to become a chief is that, there must first of all be a vacant throne to contest for by the contestants. The contestants must come from a royal lineage to the throne and must be morally upright. Thus, acts such as stealing, murder, rape, etc. are crimes that bar the involvement of a contestant from the contest. The visually impaired are also not qualified to contest. This is not an act of discrimination but rather because the gods will not be pleased with the kingmakers. He further stated that, in a situation where they are more than one contestant, an act of courtship for the throne becomes part of the traditional practice and a time period is therefore given for the courtship as the chieftaincy regalia swings from one contestant to the other during the courtship. At the end of the period, the king in consultation with his kingmakers will then select and appoint a chief from among the contestants and crown him. The chief priest is then called to come and perform a series of rituals during and after a chief has been chosen. The new chief will in turn be given the authority to also appoint those in the various communities where they reside as canton chiefs.

He told the court that historically it is a fact that the Kumus have no royal lineage to the Zotinga throne and that the Mawus started practicing chieftaincy even long before the arrival of the Kumus into Zotinga through the slave trade. He added that before 1957 and 1981 when the kumus started to lay claim to the throne, the Mawus had in succession fourteen chiefs without any dispute or conflict till the Kumus claimed they are the rightful owners of Zotinga. The lawyer concluded his submission with the strong argument that the Mawus are the rightful heir to the Zotinga throne.

"Having said all that, justices of the court, I wish to conclude by craving your indulgence to present to you the list of names of the fourteen chiefs. These are men of great honor and historical significance. They have sacrificed their lives to make this land what it is and they died here, the land where our fathers also died. Honorable justices of the court, these are the names." He tendered as evidence the names of the fourteen chiefs as follows.

1) Ali Atabia   −1721-1732
2) Alibila Atabia   −1733-1747
3) Yakubu Atabia   −1748-1753
4) Mahamadu Ali   −1754-1764
5) Mahama Mahamudu   −1765-1820
6) Baako Mahamadu   −1830-1843
7) Mamboda Mahama   −1844-1894
8) Mahama Mamboda   −1896-1908
9) Zangbeo Mamboda   −1909-1921
10) Bugri Mamboda   −1922-1935
11) Yakubu Mamboda   −1936-1950
12) Wuni Bugri Saa   −1951-1956
13) Yerimea Mahama   −1957-1966
14) Adam Zangbeo   −1967-1981

On his part, counsel for the Kumus also advanced the claim that the Kumus were the first to have settled in the land of Zotinga. He indicated that the Kumus are not challenging the rich historical accounts of the Mawus as far as the names enumerated by his learned colleague are concerned. Rather, what they want the world to understand is that the Kumus migrated from a village called Biengu in present day Burkina to their present home Zontinga many years ago before the Mawus came to join them by first settling in Pusig and later to Zotinga with the permission of the Zotinga *tindana* (land owner).

"In fact, historical records can attest to the fact that at the time the Kumus had discovered Zotinga, the Mawus by then were busy elsewhere in unknown places engaging in hunting expeditions and helping others in fighting wars." He continued, "I must also say that the Kumus acknowledges the fact that, yes, once upon a time the Mawus came to their aid when slave trade icon, Babatu used to come and forcibly capture some of our forefather and sell them to the slave raiders. We know that, but for the timely intervention of our brothers, the Mamus, possibly all of us would have been in the Whiteman's land doing plantation work at the time."

He turned and looked at some of the Mawus elders seated and teasingly smiled. "We do not deny how they helped us, but that should not be misconstrued by thinking that Zotinga is for the Mawus. Seriously I think they need to understand that the world was made to revolve and therefore, in each time period of a generation, history will be made as a continue process of human evolution. They must understand that, just as they have made enviable history, so have we also made history. Years ago it was unthinkable for our brothers the Mawus to imagine that there could ever come a time like this when the *tindanas* will reclaim their land of birth. This is a reality that they find it difficult to come to terms with. The beginning of the 20th century is ours just as they also had their time, centuries back," he told the court. He further claimed that as a matter of fact there wasn't even one settler at the time the Kumus came to Zotinga.

"Your lordships, it is worth noting that the Mawus are not saying they are the *tindanas* of Zotinga. Your lordships, a *tindan* in the Kumus dialect literally means 'land owner.' The *tindan* is the one who performs sacrifices to the gods of the land because he is the owner of the land and he acts as a chief as far as our tradition is concerned. This notion that we have never practiced chieftaincy to me is ridiculous. There has never been any Mawus in the history of this land who has ever performed any such duty of a land owner. Certainly not in Zotinga, and this is simply because they are not the *tindanas* (land owners). So, where then is the truthfulness of the claim of the Mawus that this land is for them?" In concluding his submission, he eloquently described the Mawus as just 'minority strangers' who want to rule the majority natives. He stated that the Mawus were aggressors who evaded the land of the *tindanas*.

"Your lordships, I think there is a fundamental problem with the Mawus which I just cannot understand. Legally, even though chief Bagura II is the chief of Zotinga and his name duly gazettes as such, the Mawus could only agree to refer to him as a chief of the Kumus and not Zotinga. This I think is unthinkable with no respect to the rule of law. It is unacceptable, and the court needs to take judicial notice of that." He concluded.

CHAPTER THIRTEEN

EXACTLY A FORTNIGHT after the court hearing to look into the Zotinga chieftaincy dispute, chief Bagura II sent a message to his council of elders and all the sub-chiefs under his authority, inviting them for an emergency meeting where he intended to convey to them a message from his late father chief Bagura I. They all came the next day as invited and the meeting was well attended. The palace was busy. Chief Bagura II sat right on the very arm chair his late father sat and revealed to him the 'secret' story. It was not on his traditional throne that he sat. It was just an ordinary chair which he sat on while speaking to his people.

"Elders of this land I greet you all," he greeted.

"*Naba naa, naba naa, naa, naa,*" they responded to the greetings while tenderly clapping their hands and made a little bow down to him as a show of respect. All those wearing hats had to take them off as tradition demands. After the greetings, he began to tell his sub-chiefs and elders, the message his father instructed him to tell them before he passed away.

"My elders, men of wisdom say the toad does not run in brought day light if nothing is pursuing it. It's also said that, a wise man looks for a black sheep while there is still day light. My elders and chiefs, I hope you will also agree with me that a fish which has run out of water in the pond will definitely be in trouble." He continued, "Today's meeting is therefore an important one for all of us from this land. I invited all of you here for a reason and, like the toad, the wise man and the fish as I indicated in my introduction; it goes without doubt that a meeting like this must mean something to all of us in this land. As a matter of fact and as you might all be aware by now, our continued stay in this land and on the throne is now a matter of life or death. The struggle for the throne between us the Mawus is not just a matter to be handled by the law courts. Our opponents have engaged us in an arm conflict many times before and there're all indications that, war between the two tribes may not be over anytime soon, I guess. Also, you will all agree with me that the animosity between us and our brothers and sisters the Mawus, is increasingly getting worse. We are all cousins and nephews and this land was once peaceful, prosperous, very lively and productive. In fact, we were all living happily together many, many years ago dating as far back to the days of colonialism, until after our country gained independence in 1957. I believe you all know what happened?" He paused for a while and then continued to deliver his message.

"Those of you who are well versed with our history know that my late father was made the chief of this land after we fought hard for our freedom, our land and the throne. As we are all aware, this was very possible because of our association with the party of our first President. I think we must praise the politicians among us for their foresight." There were no interruptions, no noise, no smiles as he spoke; they just listened to him talk and were waiting to hear something new from him and not what they were all aware of. They wanted him to tell them why he had summoned all of them in such short notice.

"What really could be the reason for the toad to be running in this hot sun today?" One of them whispered to the other and they all began to ponder. He continued to talk as he repositioned himself on the chair trying to make himself comfortable on the hard bamboo chair.

"My elders, from the look of current events now, we may have to ask ourselves if indeed, we can find favors from the new government in power. We all know that the new government formed is a party of the Mawus and so …"There was murmuring and nodding of heads when he drew their attention to the change of political power.

"Wise men, we therefore need to decide on our destiny as far as the right to the Zotinga throne continues to be an issue of dispute between us and the Mawus. This is one of the reasons why I called all of you here today. What then must we do?" He asked and continued to talk and paused after every sixty seconds. He explained that before the death of his father, he told him something which he need to tell them.

"My elders, I am sure we are all aware by now, that, the Mawus are bitter about everything and they have vowed never to concede defeat on this matter and are always prepared to do anything possible, to get back the throne because they believe this land is for them and not us. Certainly, we disagree with them on that issue."

"The other reason why I summoned all of you here is that, you see, in this time of our history as a people, I find it necessary and wise to let all of you know about what my late father instructed me to tell you when the time comes. I believe that this is the right time to let all of you know." He said as he cleared his throat and then stretched his left arm toward his back.

A young lady appeared and handed over a guinea fowl feather to him. It was well trimmed, leaving only part of the barb on the extreme top end. He held it in his right hand, adjusted himself on the chair one more time and rolled the feather in his right ear like a swab for about a minute and then pulled it out gently. After that, he opened his palm and gently hit the right ear three times and then continued to talk to his people.

"This message, which he told me, was many, many years ago when I was still in my youthful age. He however did warn me not to tell anyone, not even my mother or wife because it was only meant for those of us sitting here right now and that if I go contrary to his words, the gods of our land would strike me to death; my household and my generations will live with a curse." He paused and sipped some water from a calabash and continued again.

"My elders, it was an ungodly hour on that fateful day in the middle of the night and three markets days after the celebration of our maiden *samtiid* festival when he woke me up from sleep and took me to the riverside. We walked in the night through the thick grove, but he never told me anything till we got to a tall Iroko tree close to the river when he whispered to me the following words, "Stay right here my son, I will be back. Do not look right, do not look left and don't turn to your back either." He instructed, and left me there all alone as he walked away from me. He visibly walked towards the river, but the more he continue to walk away the less his visibility becomes. Suddenly a big cold wind blew over me and my eyes involuntarily closed for a few seconds. When I opened my eyes he was no more visible; he disappeared completely." They all turned and looked at each other in the faces with astonishment and some began to mumble. Bagura realized it but he could not hear what they were saying. He somehow seemed to have an idea why the whispering.

"My elders," he cleared his throat again and continued; "these are the words of our late chief to me and to you all. My late father told me he was not a Kumus as many people think, and that the throne on which he was sitting as the chief does not belong to the Kumus either. He told me he was not the rightful person to ascend to the throne. According to him, the throne was for the Mawus. Historically, they started chiefdom in Zotinga and therefore, he don't want any of his children to ascend to the throne after me. Not even my children," he added.

"Someday when you become a chief and later dead and gone, no one will be able to sit on that throne again except the rightful owners. They will surely come for it when the time is due," he told me. He further explained to me that his stay with a Mawus chief once upon a time many years ago was what made it possible for him to learn how the chieftaincy institution works as well as learn about the Mawus tradition and customary practices. Chief Bagura spoke, and everybody was voiceless. The meeting hall was quiet and silent; not even the usual noise that is always characterized with such meetings could be heard. The silence lasted for a while and died off finally. Just the nodding of heads was visible, a sign of confirmation of what they have already heard from the grapevine.

"What a revelation!!" Abila exclaimed.

Those of them who knew the history of the Kumus and Zotinga were not surprised at all. Many of the council members however, were angered upon hearing the message from no other person than their chief. They expected him to be the last person in the land to voice out such a thing. Some therefore were of the view that it was an abomination for him to have said such a thing and wanted him impeached as a chief. They believed it wasn't just an abomination, but also embarrassing and an act of betrayal. Grumbling started among them as they looked at each other.

The priest, who had been silent throughout when the chief was speaking, has now requested for his voice to be heard. He also, like many others at the meeting was not surprised at all. He knew all along this was going to happen and even warned the elders about it, but none of them paid any attention to his warning even though he is the only person they always rely on to consult the oracles or plead with the gods for pardon. He stood up and raised his head up high with his face half painted white on the right side and black on the left side. He looked up into the sky and then began to chant. He walked into a small room in the opposite direction where the chief was sitting. They could hear him loud and clear chanting but they could not understand the words. He continued to chant to invoke the spirits of the late chief Bagura I. He chanted and chanted and chanted and refused to let the gods sleep that day. He wanted them to wake up the dead body of the late chief to come and testify to what he allegedly told his son. He sounded the little drum in his hand and sang the song of the gods. The four old women who were present at the meeting joined him in singing as custom demands and the whole palace was now melodically noisy. It was a very necessary noise. Chief Bagura then woke up and walked into his room and never came back. He was not expected to come back till the priest hears from his late father. Meanwhile, a proposal was tabled for consideration and discussion. While some were of the view that the Mawus should be given what belongs to them if indeed, the revelation from the chief is true. Others also suggested that it was just better to continue fighting and defend what belongs to them after all the Mawus have declared war against them already.

"Yes, we have to fight, and we must fight. After all, all-die-be-die," one of them declared. After almost over twenty years on the throne, chief Bagura's reign had not brought out the best of Zotinga. Instead, the people have witnessed lots of conflicts, mistrust, tribalism and disunity. Tribal hatred, a senseless war and hopelessness was what many would best describe the situation in Zotinga. These traits were so deep rooted in the people that everything was now always given tribal coloration and political consideration and, despite the economic hardship and joblessness among the people, almost every household has a gun and ammunition. Anytime a violent conflict occurs in Zotinga, it becomes a nightmare to everybody. Even the religious leaders were confused and could not also comprehend the reasons why mankind would be so obsessed about terrestrial power over the desired Will of God which is, people must make the world a peaceful place and coexist as God wants it to be. As far as they are concerned, at least, they expected both tribes especially the youth, to understand this and not resort to arms at the least provocation to fight and kill.

"This is surely not what religion is expected of its followers. The people ought to know that life is a fundamental right given by God to all people and only He has the right to take it. Where have the people put religion?" A cleric questioned. Tribalism and the tendency to take to arms was so deep rooted in the people that government after government seemed helpless and hopeless in finding a lasting solution to the protracted conflict. Perhaps, the inability of government(s) to find a solution to the problem is partly because the politicians somehow benefit from it when people are divided more and more on political and tribal lines and so they rather do things that will divide the people than unite them. The human rights activists were also concerned and worried especially about the abuse of fundamental human rights of the people by the men in green uniform (the soldiers) anytime they make an arrest. The military is always merciless to the warriors anytime there was a fight in Zotinga. They have received lots of condemnation from civil society and some even called for the dismissal of those armed personnel who flocked a young teacher and naked him before his students in the very school he teaches, for allegedly possession firearm. The Human Rights activists were of the view that in as much as they recognize and appreciate the effort of the security personnel to keep peace in the area, they equally do not think the excesses committed by them were necessary and unavoidable. They appealed to the government to let equal rights and justice be seen to be done if indeed there must be peace in the area.

The peace advocates and the security expects also went from one frequency modulation station to another like a hopping mouse. They talked, explained and criticized everybody including the government for failing to act on early warning conflict signals which they have drawn the attention of the government to the situation. They also blamed the National Security and all the security agencies. Like soothsayers, they always claim to have seen the conflict looming but their warnings and advice to the appropriate bodies most often than not seemed to fall on deaf ears. They will theoretically analyze the situation very eloquently and beautifully;

suggest solutions which seemed convincing and pragmatic to the problem in Zotinga but, nothing seemed to change the mind of the very people who engages in the fight and even though everyone, including the very people fighting each other have reasons to, and are regretting for engaging in war as a means to determine who really must be on the throne, they still can't let go off their pain, forgive and stop fighting and killing each other.

The tribal rivalry between the Mawus and Kumus was increasingly getting deeper and deeper. Each one of them prefers to have its own market square, commercial lorry park, fuel stations, entertainment centers, etc. and Zotinga was now a village with two 'elephants,' and as the saying goes, when two elephants fight, it is the grass that suffers. Surely, in this case it is the innocent people that suffers when these two 'elephants' fight. The Kumus wisely adopted this strategy since most of the social amenities and other facilities, could only be found in the 'heart' of Zotinga where the Mawus predominantly occupied. They both found it necessary that way since no one from either tribe, will be spared from being lynched if he/she happens to find himself or herself at an opponent's area of control. If anyone from both sides happens to be in the wrong place at the wrong time where the presence of the military is nonexistence, then that person may not have the opportunity to live to tell his ordeal to his people. If it's a man, he will be instantly lynched to death and possibly burned with waned out car tires like a roasted chicken meat. The best treatment a woman could get for being at the wrong place were insults like 'monkey' or 'pig' depending on the tribal affiliation, or some whips on her back by little boys. These were common practices in areas where both tribes have control, and women are always the victims of this kind of treatment since they always come to the Zotinga central market to sell their farm produce. They prefer coming to that market because they cannot get people to come to their own market to trade; not even their own people.

Zotinga was now a place of discomfort to many and no one was ready or willing to migrate from any part of the country to Zotinga which was once a peaceful place and an economic hub of the country. Some of the youth from both tribes who happened to have had a progressive positive change of mind on the senseless conflict, moved to neighboring towns and many others went to the city to make a living and enjoy peace. They just don't like it and are very unhappy with the situation in their homeland, but they also find it difficult to speak their independent minds against the conflict for fear of being accused as someone who has no concern for his own people. They rather prefer to remain mute and move to other places where they could have peace but surely not without regrets of seeing their homeland been destroyed because of chieftaincy conflict. They really do not see the need or reason why they should continue to be on the path of war. Lasting peace, unity and development is what the majority of the people were desirous of, and everyone was seemingly becoming fed up with the continuous fighting. They dearly were longing for peace; the people were now looking for nothing but perfect peace.

The militant conservatives from both sides who just do not want to come to terms with a reason why they should not fight for or defend the throne, still failed to understand the value of peace. They have vowed to fight any day and any time. Unfortunately, though they take inspiration from some of the educated ones among them who encourages them to take to arms whereas they and their children will have a quiet and peaceful life outside the village devoid of being at the mercy of the security personnel who will harass them, arrest them or victimize them for allegedly engaging in the conflict. They are not directly affected by the conflict and the situation on the ground. They will assure the people of victory when they fight and tell them anything that would keep their desire to fight high. They will claim to be the liberators of the very people they instigate to take to arms and will hop from one radio station to the other telling everybody why the two tribes have been fighting for over a decade now.

"A true warrior never let his people down. He would fight in all circumstances even at the very peril of his life. A warrior will prefer to die in the battlefield than to die like a coward; he would not like to die many times before his death, but die only once. Dying in the battlefield therefore makes him the hero he is to his people just like Kpognumbu in his time who never let the king down anytime he needed him for war," one of them said.

Exactly three days after the meeting with chief Bagura II, the two tribes were at war and the Zotinga warrior led his people in the 'all-die-be-die' war and as was always the case anytime the two tribes were about to fight, a teaser gunshot was fired from Sabon-gari the night before. Then came the second gunshot. Few hours later, the third gunshot was fired also from Sabogo in responds to those being fired from Sabon-gari. Late in the night the fourth and fifth gunshots followed. These were been fired from Natinga and everybody went to sleep but were very alert for any eventualities. The next day at about 6:00 am the firing of gunshots woke everybody up and it continued from all the nine villages and, the 'all-die-be-die' war started. First, a house belonging to a Kumus near the MTTU check point was set ablaze. Then news came from one of the villages that a Mawus driver who was carrying passengers on their way to Kugri market to trade was lynched to death and set on fire together with the vehicle.

The intensity of destruction of lives and properties in that fight was unprecedented. Everybody was a victim. Innocent children were murdered in broad daylight, women were raped and chased out of their homes, houses burned to ashes and farm produce gushed down by fire. It took the military a hell of a time before they could gain ground to attempt to bring the situation under control. The situation was so alarming and the government this time decided to empower the military to take severe drastic measures aim at discouraging the people from fighting since the imposition of curfew was not yielding any good results; it couldn't deter them from fighting. Not even when the curfew hours were changed from 6:00pm to 6:00am, to 2:00pm to 10:00am could stop or even discourage them from fighting.

They fought continuously for three days and after the third day of the 'all-die-be-die' war, the warrior did not come home. He had decided to stay in the battlefield to lay ambush in the enemy's territory for undercover gorilla operation. On the forth day, a joint military and police patrol team had taken control of the streets of Zotinga even though they were still hearing sporadic shootings in some parts of the village. They decided to embark on a random operation dubbed, operation 'Where is Your Gun?' to search for fire arms and ammunition. The information about the search operation got to the warrior so, he decided not to come home. Not even on the fifth day with the aim of avoiding possible arrest from 'the men in green.'

In one of their patrols on the sixth day after the conflict, the military men saw a young man holding an M16 rifle on his back in a very charged mood. He was coming home from the battlefield. Perhaps, to tell his colleagues to prepare and join him for a night counter attack on their enemies. To their surprise, he saw them coming straight towards him from that far distance. He tried to escape by running into an uncompleted building to hide. From that distance, he thought the security personnel in the camouflage armed car never saw him. He remained in the building until he could not see the car anymore then he jumped over a wall into another room. There again he jumped over through another window. This time around he jumped outside the building from the second room. Unknowingly to him, two military men had already taken cover close to the building when they saw him run into it. Outside the building, he stood there for a while, and then carefully looked to his left side and straight on the road to see if the armed men in uniform were coming. He did not see any moving vehicle or human being on the other opposite side of the road from where he was standing and was therefore, convinced it was now safe for him to escape from the sight of the patrol team. But then, he didn't. He decided to sit down and reload his spare magazine in readiness to fight just in case he was under attack by the enemy.

To his surprise also, the two armed men suddenly appeared from the opposite directions where he least expected and quickly he was disarmed and arrested without him putting up any resistance. They took him to the military camp where Captain Frank apparently was having a meeting with the junior ranks to map out an operational strategy to facilitate in bringing the situation to a perfect control alongside with the ongoing operation 'Where Is Your Gun'

At the military camp, Frank asked him why he wasn't in school but instead, was out there risking his life in such a senseless fight at this tender age. The young man was mute. He only stared at him showing total deportment of pain, anger and disregard to how the military feels about him or would want to treat him.

"Will you stop looking at me and answer my question, 'small'?" Frank calmly spoke to the warrior in a civilian tone with a friendly face just to make him feel relaxed, less tense and comfortable to talk to him. He didn't answer the question. He again raised his head and look into the captain's eyes with a mean face.

"What is your name, small?" He asked his second question but the man never uttered a word. "Listen to me small boy, I have asked you questions and you wouldn't mind me. Are you dumb?"

"No." he uttered his first word and stared at the captain again.

"What is your name, I say?" He asked the question for the second time but no answer.

"Can't you hear me? I'm asking you what your name is." Frank was beginning to lose his temper but, he managed to control his emotions. The boy stared at him again and then answered, "I am the warrior."

"What! The captain exclaimed and queried. "I'm asking you your name and you're here telling me you're the warrior? Oh I see. So, it's you who have been leading your people in the war and telling them not to stop fighting?" Frank turned and looked at his colleague soldiers.

"Can you all imagine this?" He asked and then took a few steps away from the boy. He walked angrily to the window behind him and gazed briefly at the four soldiers standing in the foyer and then back to the warrior. One of the men who arrested him stepped forward and gave a salute.

"Okay my dear warrior as you call yourself, so, where did you get this gun from and who taught you how to use it?" The warrior didn't answer the question. He rather asked the captain a series of questions. "Sir," he began to speak. "I don't care whatever you may do to me now that I'm in your custody. But let me also ask you these questions and until somebody is able to provide me and my people some answers, we will forever continue to fight even when I'm dead and gone."

Sir, these are my questions which I would like to get answers. What would you do if your opponent destroy your home, threaten your future, stole your freedom, killed your brother or father, where will you draw the line? What would you do if they suppressed and oppressed your people? What would you do if the government refuses you your fundamental rights to celebrate you cultural heritage or deny you justice? If they seized your farmland and killed your son, your mother, cousin or anybody dear to you, if they killed your colleague warrior or burned your house, what would you do? What will you all do if they killed a brother at the Mosque, lynched your uncle or massacre your family? You see I'm a small boy but I know that this village was discovered by my great, great, great grandparents many, many years ago and I will fight the enemy till I get back what belongs to us. Frank looked at him and then smiled.

"Have you heard of Christopher Columbus before? He asked.

"No sir," he answered.

"Well, I think that you people, I mean both tribes are acting like Christopher Columbus who said he is the one who discovered Africa." All the soldiers laughed but the warrior didn't. To him there was nothing funny to laugh about. Frank did not answer any of his questions. He only ordered his men to treat him as he calls himself and walked away.

"Well, guys," he said he is the unknown warrior. So, I think you should handle him as such," he instructed and turned to walk away. But, before he could close the door as he walked out from the room, a swift and unexpected electrifying slap was given to the warrior, forcing him to fall flat on the floor and began screaming for help. "Captain, captain, captain," he called and cried. The pain was very severe so he cried and cried and cried. Nevertheless, he made sure he spoke his mind.

"I was born a warrior and I shall die a warrior. I will fight till I kill all of them," he angrily said. After disciplining him reasonably with some slaps, the soldiers then took him far away to the cemetery late in the evening where they showed him graves of all those who died in all the conflicts. They pointed to him one after the other graves on the ground saying, "this one you see here was a warrior before you. The other one over there was a Kumus and that one in front of you was a Mawus. Have you seen this one, right there?" The colonel asked him and pointed his finger to a grave at the far end under a tree.

"That grave there is the grave of a teacher who was murdered in cold blood on his way home from a peace meeting just because of his love to see peace so that people like you could have education and a better future. But what happened, this innocent man was lynched and stoned to death by charlatans like you."

After showing him the graves, they left him there standing at the cemetary as they walked to the car. The driver motioned the vehicle and within a distance of about fifty meters away from where the warrior was standing, one of the soldiers aimed at him and pulled the trigger of the M16 gun. A bullet sprout like a spear with high velocity and pierced through his forehead. The second bullet went into his chest and he fell down instantly dead.

CHAPTER FOURTEEN

THE FOLLOWING DAY Zotinga was unusually quiet and calm. In the morning of that Wednesday, the youth from both tribes had grouped at their bases discussion about the aftermath of the war and recounting what had happened on the battlefield. The Mawus counted number of Kumus they have killed, and the number of houses they have burned to ashes. The Kumus also seemed happy. They claimed to have killed many of the Mawus this time around; more than any of the conflicts they both fought.

News about his where about began to spread very fast all over like dry season bush fire but none of them could tell if he was alive or dead. The next day it was lingering in the rumor mail that the warrior was killed in the war. The Kumus were quick to pride themselves for killing him. They were happy to hear that he was dead though they never saw his dead body. Some however were still skeptical about the news till they heard that Bachela had come from the city to join in mourning with the victims of the conflict. He was very sad about the situation and also about the death of the warrior who did not heed to his advice. He remembered he had advised him and many of his colleagues from both tribes the last time he was in the village, urging them to stop fighting. He vividly remembered admonishing the warrior in particular and sundry to stop this senseless war and begin to give peace a chance.

"Yesterday it was one of them. Today it's one of us. Tomorrow it could be me or you. It could be a mother, a father, a son, a student, a child, a farmer. It could be anyone. So, when will we all rise up and say goodbye to tribal conflict? Why must we continue to fight when none of us have been able to win any of the wars that we have been fighting? In this time and era wars are not a means of determining a victor; no. Surely not like in the days of our great, great forefathers when survival and superiority of a tribe or people were largely dependent on fighting to conquer," he told the crowd gathered. It was a mass funeral organized for all the victims who died in the conflict.

"The Mawus have never been able to strip off the chieftaincy crown from chief Bagura II in any of the wars neither has the Kumus been able to drive out the Mawus from this land since the beginning of this conflict; not even in the recent all-die-be-die conflict. My brothers and sisters, in all these wars, our chief has always survived. Those of us who are outside this land and leaving elsewhere also always survived these wars, but is it the same with those of you who are in it? Can we say that about those of you who go out to fight? Can we say we are all safe? No, surely not. What happens then? Rather, it is those of you who go out to fight that are killed. It's you and me. So, why must we continue to fight?" Everybody was quiet and very attentive. They listened and watched him talk as he admonished them. His words pierced through their veins like cold blood and they began to shiver inwardly. "Who loses or wins anytime we fight? No one wins, but rather all of us from this land loses," he ended his torchy speech, and everybody was still mute. They just nodded their heads in agreement to the entire speech. He spoke as if it were a sermon.

The astute young attorney was deeply saddened about the effects of the conflict on his people and for the past one year, after the 'all-die-be-die' war, he has been talking to everybody and anybody he could reach out to. Pleading, persuading and admonishing them to understand that no matter how they all look at the situation, no matter how deep hatred they all have for each other, and no matter the tribal interest at stake, they could never be anything useful, beautiful and beneficial to anybody and everyone in the community and to humanity than living together in peace and using nonviolence means to resolve any differences as a people. As the lead attorney for the Mawus, he believed that the rule of law must be allowed to take its normal course. As a Mawus himself and inasmuch as he believed that chief Bagura and the Kumus cannot continue to claim that Zotinga is for them and that they are the rightful heirs to the throne, he also strongly believes that as far as the law remains as it is now, Bagura is legally the chief and ought to be accepted as such by all till otherwise decided by the law courts.

He therefore, decided to initiate a crusade to champion the course of peace as a progressive minded generational thinker who does not believe that tribal war is the answer to the problem at hand. He believes that all of them as a people must learn to give peace a chance to flourish in the land so that they could all together rebuild and reshape the destiny of their homeland and stop taking pride in killing each other. "We are in a world today that is ruled by knowledged based power; where education counts and not the symbolism of being a chief or, the number of stock piled of arms and ammunitions. Thus, we have to redirect our resources, energy and time in education if we want to remain relevant to our communities and dominate or have control of the affairs. Guns do not rule the world any longer. So therefore, the only path for all of us is to join a world of peace where the rule of law dictates the order of the day," he said.

His view on the way forward as far as the situation in Zotinga was concerned, is for the two tribes to embraced nonviolence means of solving their differences by themselves and also respecting the rule of law because it is the same law that they are seeking to use to get the throne back. However, even though his views and understanding of the issue at stake between his tribe's men and the Kumus could be criticize by some as being naïve, his views were realistically reasonable. Nonetheless, it was a daring risk he had embarked upon for holding such views; a risk of being labeled as a conformist of an injustice system which they believe favors the desire of the Kumus. A risk of being considered an outcast for suggesting that chief Bagura should be recognize by all as the chief of the land. A risk of abandonment for concentrating much of his advocacy on the need for peace without echoing the injustices his people are suffering from the government. It was a risk of facing dejections and rejection from his people despite the many times he has raised his voice high and loud enough in the law courts, radio stations and even sometimes on political platforms all towards the struggle to reclaim the throne from the Kumus. Nonetheless, as far as the majority of his people are concerned, it is unthinkable for anyone and especially for him in particular being their lawyer to even consider that a Kumus chief should be accepted and recognized as a chief of Zotinga, till the law courts decide otherwise.

"My brothers and sisters, it is time we all work together and put an end to this conflict. You see, it seemed we are all underestimating the effect of the conflict on our lives for the past two decades. This is a conflict that has caused us to kill each other, hate each other, mistrust each other etc. This is a conflict that has brought hopelessness in the youth for a brighter future. Our youths are jobless. Very disturbing is the fact that it has affected education in this part of the country. Some of our farmers also can't farm on their farmlands because either the farms have been confiscated by Kumus or that the safety of their lives can't be guaranteed. Our children can't go to school for fear of being lynched to death. Our fathers and mothers can't travel to nearby villages to trade for fear of being murdered. All these are concerns that should let us think twice."

"The fundamental problem with both of us, the Mawus and the Kumus is that we seemed to have clouded our minds only on chieftaincy—something that continually loses its relevance in this time and age. My brothers and sisters do not get me wrong on this issue. I believe in tradition and for that matter the chieftaincy institution but, I really think that it is about time we start thinking and looking beyond chieftaincy if we are to make this land a better home for our children just as our parent did for us. It is very disheartening sometimes to note that, our children born a decade ago in this land do not know what peace is; they came to this land only knowing war, a conflict that destroys them. Yes we could also talk about injustices, tribalism, favoritism, and all other issues that affects peace building, but my brothers and sisters, must that be enough reason not to work for peace?" He questioned and paused for a while and then continued to talk. He was lucky to have caught the undivided attention of the people. No one disrupted his long speech of peace even though some totally disagreed with him on some of his views. He could notice it in their faces but somehow that never demoralized him because he knew that there were many others also who understood him very well on his views but chose to remain silent.

Two days later after he had spoken to the youth from both tribes, he met the Mawus Youth Association on the way forward for Zotinga. "I do not believe in war, and I know many of you do not also believe in using conflict to resolve the chieftaincy dispute. I believe in law and order. I believe in peace and harmony and I believe in love for one another and justice for all. As a lawyer who believes in the rule of law, I must say that I will use the law to fight for what belongs to us and we the Mawus will do everything legally possible to win the case. We will continue to press on the government and the powers that be to allow the funeral of our late chief to be performed as custom demands and for the sake of crossing the bridge to obtaining peace. He died as a chief of this land and not a commoner and he must be regarded as such and his funeral performed," he told them.

It rained and everywhere was muddy that day. It was the first rain of the new farming season and everybody was happy especially the farmers. The crowd was thick at the forecourt of the late chief Zangbeo's palace. Despite the overwhelming muddy nature of the ground, the people came to listen to the message. Bachela was expected to come and speak to his people. It was his second time just a few days after he spoke to the youth. They rather preferred to be in the rain till the lawyer comes to break the news to them. They waited for him, standing in the muddy ground. Few minutes' later news went around that Bachela was coming to inform them about the decision of the court on the chieftaincy dispute. It was speculated that the president had given the green light for the Mawus to perform the funeral of the late chief Zangbeo. Indeed, it's said that he had communicated to the elders and requested that a meeting be called immediately so that he could explain directly to everyone about the new development on the matter.

In the afternoon of that Saturday, he came to the palace. Even though he was expecting a good number of people to converge at the palace ground, the crowd he saw was unprecedented; one would not be far from right should he compared it to a political rally. Those who couldn't find places to stand to have a good view of who would be speaking to them had to climb on trees and some on walls and roof tops just to have a glimpse of the speakers and to hear what was going to be said. Everyone was eager with anticipation and almost everybody talked and speculated on what was going to be said. The speculation continued as everybody was into it. Some claimed to have heard from reliable sources about what they were speculating. Others just advanced their speculation nicely. They speculated as if really a date for performing the funeral was what the elders were to decide. There was excitement in the crowd. It was an excitement of a sign of hope and victory. Soon after the elders had finished addressing them, the young attorney was called to deliver his message to the people. Bachela stood up and walked to the middle of the crowd. He stood there for a minute without saying anything. Then he turned around and glanced at the people and then requested a minute silence in remembrance of the departed souls who died in the conflict. After that he began to speak and in his usual soft and sharp voice he said, "My elders and leaders of our great tribe I greet you all."

"We greet you too." The crowd responded.

"My brothers and sisters, our mothers and everyone present I greet you all and I thank you for responding to the call of our wise men in such a short notice. As a matter of fact, I believe most of you here remember or know very well that there is a big problem in this our land and that is, the chieftaincy dispute between us and our brothers the Kumus. I believe you are all also aware that we have taken the matter to court." The crowd was very attentive and unruffled and the whole area was peaceful and quiet.

He continued, "Well, one of the news I have for all of you today is that, three months ago we took the chieftaincy matter to the law court and the court has critically looked into the matter and taken a conclusive decision. The court decided that the matter should be handled by the National House of Chiefs. The quietness immediately disappeared when he told them the case was referred to the NHC. They clapped hands and many were smiling. At least they believed that the NHC knows about the historical facts about the Zotinga throne very well and therefore will be the right institution to decide on the matter. They have always believed that a decision on the matter will be in their favor.

"I hope you will all remember that sometime ago right here in this palace I made it clear to all of you that the legal battle for our claim regarding this issue is not over yet, and our opponents will have to meet us in the law court someday sooner or later. I also remember assuring all of you that this year's annual *damba* festival will surely be celebrated as planned. Can you remember that? He asked with smiles beaming on his face. The crowd answered with joy, saying, "Yes we do. You told us so."

"Well, right now as I'm standing here before our elders and before you all, the good news I have for all of us here as a tribe is that, first, the court have also directed that before the NHC will look into the matter and decide on it, the funeral of our late chief, Zangbeo must be performed since there're records indicating that he was one of the many people who ruled Zotinga as a chief and died when he was still a chief but his funeral was not performed since he passed away. A letter to that effect has been written to the father of the land, our president and in my hand right now is a copy of the letter." Again, the crowd clapped in a jubilant mood.

He continued. "The good news here is that, the government will soon issue a white paper to that effect." He paused for a short while and continued. "My brothers and sisters, the other good news which our elders have asked me to share with all of you here is that, our application to the police to celebrate our annual *damba* festival for this year has been approved. Our elders are yet to decide on a date." The whole place was now engulfed with noise as the people shouted with joy, horns were trumpeted and people screamed on top of their voices in happiness. It was great news and a great day for them. The evening was drawing closer and Bachela was eager to conclude his speech after telling them all what they needed to know. But the crowd cared less about time; there were prepared to stay there as long as the elders wanted to talk to them.

"My dear brothers and sisters, this is the reason why our elders have summoned us here. Having said all that, one thing which we must all understand is that none of our hopes and dreams and or the good news that I just shared with you will happen if we continue to fight. Without peace, we cannot do anything; there will not be development and there will not be prosperity. So, we must embrace peace as a first step. My dear brothers and sisters, I will therefore entreat all of you to embrace peace and eschew any act that could ignite another conflict and disturb our planned activities. There is too much blood on this land already. Come to think of it, are we not intermarried? So why must we continue to allow that togetherness to get destroyed?" He asked.

"I am not saying this because I am a coward, but I am thinking of the lives we lose every time we fight. Let is even think about the suffering our farmers go through. They cannot go to their farms to do farming activities just because of the fear of being attacked or killed. Our widows cannot have the peace of mind after losing their husbands. Our children cannot have a father. Who will tell me if there is anyone of us here who is a stranger to this our situation? No one, we all know how it started and how far we have come ever since our first fight. Who at all does not know what the government did to us in 1958? Who does not know how Zotinga started and who does not know about the war?" He asked, and everybody was silent. The jubilation immediately ceased. He spoke with passion and sincerity. He continued to talk to the people with the ultimate hope that he will be understood and not misunderstood.

"The situation is always unbearable anytime we fight. It really does not matter who started it. What should really be a matter of concern is when are we going to stop this fighting if not now?" He paused, and stood there looking around to see if anyone will have the answer to the question. The crowd was still mute. No one volunteered to answer the question and no one asked a question either. Then he continued to speak.

"My dear brothers and sisters, these are my answers to the question I asked. It's an answer of hope. It is a dream. The dream is a dream that comes with hopes and aspirations for all of us in this land including the Mawus and the Kumus as well as all the other tribes. It is a dream that is deep rooted on the principles and beliefs, that togetherness includes our desire for absolute peace, unity, forgiveness, and love for one another. We must therefore endeavor to build trust among us as a first step," he said and continued.

"As I said, this dream is for all of us and we must all spread the message. It comes with a pledge from all of us, that, as much as the significance of tribal belongingness and political affiliation cannot be wish away but value by all, we also must work hard to break the barriers of tribalism and uproot tribal discrimination and strive to live together in one true spirit as one people with equal rights, justice and a common destiny as was the case during the days of our forefathers. The politicians of this land must also stop the stock piling of weapons to train people to become guerilla fighters, as reported in the newspapers with the photos of these trainees. Our governments must have the political will to deal decisively on serious issues like this and the security agencies must step up vigilance and endeavor to make arrest. The governments must act to stop this. My brothers and sisters, the dream also comes with the individual belief and hope of the possibility of achieving prosperity, success and happiness, and that life should be better for all with opportunities for each one according to his/her ability or achievement regardless of which political party or tribe one belongs to or, the circumstances of that person." He paused again for a while and continued.

"Indeed, we must understand that each of us is endowed by God with among other rights, the right to life and the pursuit of his/ her God given talent in a peaceful environment with happiness. Essentially, this dream envisages that our children can live together peacefully and have the opportunity to better their lives through education no matter our difference or tribal interest, and that we are determined to use peace as a tool to give true meaning to this dream of hope. The idealistic vision and goal of this dream is that no individual or tribe would be discriminated, against based on political or tribal reasons. The goal of this dream, my brothers and sisters, is to take cognizance of our political, ethnic, tribal and cultural diversity and unite for the good of our homeland. We must therefore continue to extend a handshake of peace to our opponents and accept one from them if they do extend it to us. This dream comes with the hope that both tribes will, sooner or later hold hands again and walk together on our streets in a true spirit of peace and unity as it used to be 200 years ago, and in the recent past before our first conflict. We must therefore continue to extend a peace handshake to our opponents and accept one from them if they do extend it to us. Thank you," he concluded.

Drums began to sound and the orator recited almost all the praises due him. The elders also joined the crowd to clap in giving their approval to everything the orator was saying about Bachela. "You are indeed a true son of this land like your father," one of them said to him.

CHAPTER FIFTEEN

ONE EARLY MONDAY morning on the ninth day of the ninth month, and a year after the funeral of the late chief was announced, the sun was seen rising at the usual time but not in its usual color. It was white and the rays were bright; shining on the whole village and the people could see a reflection of a shadow of the warrior in their mind's eye. It was a reminder of victory and the end of tribal conflict in the village and a new beginning.

The day appeared foggy, but all had gathered that day to join the Mawus give a befitting burial to their late chief. The funeral ground was just about 2km away from the P&T office where the 'aflao niggers' usually sit. The 'niggers' as they are known, are a group of individuals mainly the youth who happened to have had the opportunity one way or the other to have traveled to the city and therefore, had the opportunity to experienced city life like Awule and Lion. They are a section of the youth who have decided to embrace western life style, especially the American one which they have learned from the city, and they made sure they took advantage of all the pride that goes with traveling to the city and distinct themselves from the rest in the village. None of them however have ever been to America, but most of the time they walk, dress, cut their hair and even talk like Americans. They were present at the funeral and were as usual, recognizably different from the rest in their dressing and the ladies love to see them. They really admire them.

Later in the day after all the people had gathered at the funeral ground, the priest unceremoniously appeared from nowhere after the customary rites had been performed, to kick start the funeral. He walked in a backward direction into the crowd and stood in the middle. He walked from one end to the other chanting and singing. In every three steps that he took he would pause and chant and then move again and stop, swinging back and forth. Repeatedly, he did so for about fifteen steps before stabilizing himself right in the middle of the crowd again. The elders and the royal family where seated and watching; they were the only people who knew and understood the essence of the calculated fifteen steps the priest took as he walked back and forth in front of them. They also knew that the priest was consulting the oracles to know which of the many contestants from among all the five royal gates will be chosen by the gods as the next chief after the funeral. He raised his head up high and looked into the sky, watching the appearance of the sun. He chanted and chanted and chanted and then gave a vociferous shout forcing the sun to shoot out from the sky in its full size. He then turned to the elders and said to them.

"There is a stranger among you in this land and the gods are angry. That is why the sun did not rise in its true colors. Do you know who the stranger is?" He asked. They were all mute. He asked again, for the second and then third time.

"Do you know who that person is?" The crowd was quiet, and none spoke. None of the elders answered him either.

"Okay, this is the message from the gods. According to the gods, there is a stranger in the land who cannot be a chief of this land. This is why the gods are very angry and when the gods of the land become angry, then calamity will surely befall the people. No wonder you people have been fighting and killing each other for the past two decades now," he paused for a while and then continued to deliver the message as revealed by the oracle. "The gods are really angry and according to the oracles, the 'stranger' among you migrated with his parents from Duutinga to Pusig where they were received by one of the descendants of the late king and were given free land to settle and farm. While there as a domestic servant to the chief he was responsible for taking care of the stables. The gods acknowledged that he was a good and obedient servant to the chief and was so happy with his family in Pusig, but things turned sour when he abused the privileges his parents had from the royal family. He was therefore banished from Pusig and was received in Zotinga after he confessed his crime to the chief at that time and pleaded for protection. His plea was accepted by the chief of this land at the time out of sympathy, and he hosted him in his house. The descendant of this stranger according to the oracles, was a chief and his offspring also wants to be the chief of this land and the gods are truly angry." He told the crowd that gathered to witness the burial ceremony. The Kumus were also present and they delivered a solidarity message on the need for peacefully coexistence from chief Bagura.

Few years after the funeral was performed, everybody in Zotinga suddenly became happy. The loss of hope and mistrust for over a decade, the killings and hurting each other because of chieftaincy was now giving way for peaceful coexistence after a long break of ethnic violence.

Everybody was simply happy and nobody wanted to be left out of the joy. All seem delighted including the Kumus. The wars and conflicts they fought against each other, the killings of innocent children and women, all the wounds afflicted on their souls and the many atrocities and murders that occurred in the land, the hatred and vengeance they had against each other, the sense of superiority and inferiority against each other, were gone. It all vanished, and chieftaincy was not the ultimate to them anymore; certainly not when the authority of a chief on any matter could be challenged by the people in the law courts with no fear.

The early hours of the next day witnessed a heavy down pour of rain and throughout that week everything seemed good and, everyone was happy. The next day, the weather was cloudy, but with less chance of rain. The sun appeared late in the morning but was not as hot as it normally would be at that time. The combination of the clouds and the sun was evenly distributed by midday giving the people a very pleasant weather temperature for a beautiful day. Indeed, it was a lovely day. The Mawus were once again happy and so were the Kumus also and everyone else in the land. Perhaps, their hard work of taking the responsibility to work to achieved peace among themselves and by themselves, might have given them a feeling of pride, propelled by the audacity of hope which the youth had in believing that achieving peace in their homeland was not impossible, but it has to start with each and every one of them. Probably this is what made them feel very happy about a prosperous future of togetherness.

The preceding Thursday was characterized with thunders and no one could dare come out. Two days after, a 'peace durbar' was organized and all the tribes involved participated. The durbar was a symbolic event to mark the beginning of peace and reconciliation between the Kumus and the Mawus, and to mark an end of over a decade of blood spillage on the land. It was also meant to solidify the peace and unity journey initiated three years ago by the youth, and all the ethnic tribes were at the durbar and many others from across the country were invited to join in the celebration. A land mark of history was to be made. The peace durbar was a celebration of forgiveness, love, happiness, harmony and peaceful coexistence.

The Mawus came with their chief and elders and the Kumus also came with their chief and elders and it was just an electrifying moment of joy at the Community Centre. No one had laid ambush with any weapon to disturb the durbar; it was just a happy and unity day. They all came in their numbers; they sang peace songs and dance to their traditional songs. The streets were dense with merry throngs of the youth in their beautiful attires meant for the occasion. The day was full of pleasantries, handshakes, eating, sharing etc. They played games and everybody was absolutely happy and satisfied with each other, and the durbar ended peacefully.

The following year after the durbar, there was perfect peace; absolute enough for them to be happy and proud of their effort. It was the kind of peace that they needed. The past glorious days known of Zotinga, not war or hatred. It was just peace, understanding and togetherness. The future was bright and promising for generations to come. They have finally gotten the peace they had hoped and longed for. They got it through their own hard work and the will to forgive and built a happy home for generation yet to come. The Mawus and the Kumus were now united more than ever before. In one of his meetings with the elders from both tribes, Bachela made a proposal for the annual celebration of the peace and unity durbar where the two chiefs from both tribes and their people will meet to celebrate their efforts and continue to forgive each other and consolidate peace.

May 20, a year after the second anniversary of the peace and unity durbar celebration, the two tribes once again came together to celebrate the third anniversary of peaceful coexistence, and as has always been the case, the durbar ground was packed with people and the crowd was lively. It was full of pageantry and the usual exhibition of their diverse rich cultural heritage. The people interacted among themselves to solidify their unity and peace. Again, it was to mark a turning point in the history of Zotinga, and people came from all walks of life to witness and be part of the history making moment; celebration of the third anniversary of the end of a two decades of tribal armed conflicts. Everyone indeed was happy. They were happy perhaps, because the Kumus and the Mawus are now at peace with each other, with a genuine heart to finally say goodbye to war. They were all happy because no one would have ever believed that they could ever be a day in the history of Zotinga when the two protagonists in the conflict would accept to bury their chieftaincy and tribal differences and talk about peace and unity with a genuine heart.

Pleasantries were shared among all of them and merrily, they showed true happiness and forgiveness to each other for coming this far. Rightly so, they were happy because this marks a new beginning of lasting peace and the end of tribal unrest. Farmers can now go to their farms without the fear of being attacked. The women can also go to the market without the fear of being lynched. The children can now go to school, and the government also could now channel the monies spent on peace keeping and develop the village. They were all happy because there was no loser in this new course they have chosen. Everyone was a winner, the hatred and suspicion they had against each other had now gone forever. They could now trust each other and work together as one people. These and many other reasons were sufficient for all to smile about, and pat each other on the shoulder for embracing peace. It was all about hope and joy boldly written on the faces. It was a goodbye to tribal conflict. It was a new day, a new peace, a new people and a new beginning.